Elites

Chloe Porter

Contents

00 | the girl with the red lips

----

he who seeks revenge should remember to dig two graves.□

[Chinese Proverb]

Preface: The girl with the red lips

"HELLO," SHE SAID with a sugary smile that would've seemed fake if she didn't have a branding of the high school sweetheart, but I had my doubts. "You must be the new girl."

Her hair was a type of blonde that made me ponder if it was made out of actual gold and her eyes were stunningly cobalt, almost as bright as the sky, blinking with curiosity as she examined me (not so subtly, if I may add), possibly speculating if I could potentially be the next candidate to their little game. It briefly reminded of a time a few summers ago where I was out for a swim at my best friend's home in the Hamptons, and a squeal caused a flock of birds to take off in shock.

"You wouldn't believe what just happened," My best friend said with excitement lacing in her voice as she rushed out from the house, waving a piece of paper around in the air. I raised a brow expectantly; waiting for her to indulge me with whatever news she had this time round. "I've been invited to the bonfire at the beach tomorrow evening!"

She squealed again, her eyes wide and wild with anticipation. I felt a slight pang of irritation, but I said nothing, not wanting to diminish my best friend's happiness. Instead, I pretend that I understood her high society life and grinned.

"Oh my god," I replied, trying to match the same amount of enthusiasm she was expressing. "I'm so happy for you!"

Suddenly, her grey eyes narrowed seriously, her red lips frowning slightly as she watched me get out of the pool and dry up. "You don't know how serious this is, do you?"

I smiled sheepishly at her and she groaned in annoyance, throwing her head. Sometimes, I wondered what went through her mind when she realised, I would never be like the people she wanted to impress. She could deny it all she wanted but I knew her. I knew my best friend.

"Listen to me, Candy," she began, her crimson lips beaming. Red always suited her, never took my liking. "These events are only given to those who could potentially be the next protégée for Celeste Leon. It's so exclusive, not even the Jenner's could get an invite."

"So, essentially, what you're doing here is basically a try–out to be the next servant for a rich privileged bitch?"

"Excusez-moi, you're talking to one right now," she snapped, surprising me with her harsh tone. "Or am I not rich enough to fit in that category?"

I frowned, furrowing my brows in utter confusion, "Scar, I didn't mean to offend you. I was just saying. These were the types of people we used to make fun of."

Scarlett Lockwood stood up, rolling her eyes in aversion and for a moment, I doubted if I knew my best friend. She looked the same as she did yesterday, and the day before, and the day before that day. Auburn coloured hair, grey feline eyes and sprinkles of freckles on her high cheekbones, which were glittered with highlight and blush, enhancing her signature red lips. Yes, she looked the same.

Or maybe she didn't.

Maybe I wasn't looking close enough —

"That was like in eighth grade, C. We don't do that anymore," Huffing in exasperation, she sashayed off in her new Jimmy Choo's, snapping my attention back onto the situation at hand. "Whatever, I'll catch you later."

"What about your mother's benefit tonight?" I shouted before she disappeared into the large house. She didn't even glance over her shoulder when she gave me a reply.

"I won't be going to that. Just tell her I'm not feeling well. She'll understand."

And as she sauntered away, I wish I went after her. Or with her at least. But how was I meant to know that was going to be the beginning of her downfall.

The people she was in love with were Gods to her; she worshipped their very existence and everything that came with them. They were the worst types of people; unreasonably wealthy, stunning and wicked. Yet, they seemed to capture everyone's attention. They were Elites and they knew it. They knew they were the very sun of our little solar system and because of it, they had everyone's fascination. Scarlett wanted that. She wanted to be them. She's always liked the spotlight and attention along with the devotion that came along with it. But she wasn't them; she could never be them no matter how much she tried. To them, she was a black sheep trying to find its way back to the flock and that made her vulnerable, exposed.

And when they knew every inch of her weaknesses, it wouldn't be long until they said checkmate.

However, one thing that constantly haunted me at the back of my mind was her sudden change of heart. I still didn't understand where it wrong, where along the lines did she switch and decide to go rogue. Scarlett was a beautiful girl, and I had never met a girl so beautiful yet so complex. Not that it mattered anymore. What was done was done. I wanted them to pay, them to feel exactly how Scar felt when they embarrassed her at the Winter Formal during Junior Year.

I wanted to carve the rejection into their labels and titles the same way they did to Scarlett. I wanted them to be so vulnerable that no matter how much money they spent on burying their secrets, they'd always know that someone out there knew the truth behind their wealthy façade and was waiting to dig up their graves.

And it began right then. Senior year. By the time I was done with them, I'd have avenged every innocent person they hurt just for entertainment, especially Scarlett.

"Are you okay?" The beautiful blonde asked with a look of concern painted on her face when I didn't answer her, perhaps reconsidering if I could be a candidate or not.

I smiled, my lips painted red, "Perfect."

01 | solar systems

Chapter I: Solar Systems

Hi Scarlett,

I finally had the pleasure of seeing this so-called Queen of Harrington. She isn't as beautiful as you made her out to be. I was expecting some kind of goddess. I was sadly disappointed.

Still don't understand your obsession with Celeste Leon. You destroyed yourself trying to live to her standard which was apparently 'perfect' in Harrington: thin, popular, rich. I can almost picture you are sitting with them, laughing with them, being with them but at the same time not being there. Who were you actually, Scarlett?

Wish me luck; I'm going to need it.

Sent by Candace at 6:00 P.M.

***

IF HARRINGTON was a solar system, Celeste Leon would be the sun, the centre of the galaxy. The planets that orbit her would be the rest of the Elites, some closer to her than others. Everyone else were the pesky stars that would never achieve the same power as them. She wasn't this exquisite beauty that everyone had depicted her out to be. Her swirly, ebony hair and plump lips coated in a rosy tint was all part of her act. When she smiled, it was forced, her eyes wouldn't crinkle and there was this certain coldness that flickered through them.

Yet, she was all.

Life at Harrington revolved around her.

The students at this school practically bowed down to her without questioning why, she had everyone wrapped around her finger and, with a flick of her wrist, she could destroy them too.

Indubitably, the goddess sat in the middle of the table besides Madeline Vos, the high school sweetheart, a cup of coffee clutched in her perfectly manicured hand. Celeste laughed daintily at something the blonde bombshell whispered to her when a freshman skittered past them uneasily. It only made me hate them more.

It was no brainer that Madeline was truly like Celeste, but her reputation of being the 'high school sweetheart' said otherwise and that bothered me; I couldn't wait until I proved everyone wrong. See, what annoyed me was how charismatic and perfectly primped Celeste was; she was the embodiment of grace and charisma. You couldn't help but like her or even worse, admire her.

I sat on the floor above them on an empty table on the mezzanine which overlooked the cafeteria. It was the perfect location to stay hidden from everyone, especially the Elites. It was where Scarlett once sat when she first came to this school. I remember her telling me all about the amazing view it had of the cafeteria or, more like, the Elites.

"The view is the best on the mezzanine," Scar grinned, shifting her focus momentarily away from her nail that she was painting to me. "I didn't discover it until my second week there, I wish I saw it earlier. Who knows what I could've uncovered?"

I guess she was right.

Sat on the left of Celeste was Bentley Harrington, the only one insane enough to date her for a grand total of three years and 10 months. He was what people called the 'male version of Celeste'. His dark brown hair was neatly pushed back, revealing haunting brown eyes which scoured the cafeteria before paying attention meticulously to his other half.

As the grandson of the very founder of this school, Bentley consequently owned everyone that breathed in this building, which made Celeste an eminently powerful Queen. Being the heir of nearly half of the skyscrapers across the globe, their relationship was plastered on every newspaper and source of media across the city, not only cementing the partnership between her mother and his father, but claiming their right to the throne which waited for them, their names engraved in gold.

He held her other hand, more possessively than affectionately, resting it on the table for the rest of the cafeteria to see him claiming what he owned. The two were the ultimate power couple and if anyone dared to hurt his queen, off with their heads.

"I heard you guys went Europe," Madeline questioned, grinning teasingly at the pair. "Didn't know you were such a romantic, Bentley."

Bentley replied back with cold smirk, "What can I say, sis? She just brings the best out of me."

Madeline scowled at her stepbrother, crossing her arms over her chest in displeasure. Their relationship not being a surprise to me as over summer, the marriage between Esme Vos and Darius Harrington was seen on every tabloid in New York and, possibly, across the world. It was physically unavoidable. Clearly, Madeline hated their new status more than Bentley, or maybe he enjoyed tormenting her with reminders that she and he were family. It wouldn't be surprising if it was the latter.

"And who might you be?"

I failed to stop myself from jumping when the presence of an unfamiliar body positioned themselves next to me at the table. I clenched my jaw before plastering the best false smile I could master to the culprit that interrupted my thoughts; a skill I became a quick expert at when hanging around Scarlett. With short curly chestnut hair and grey eyes which curiously, yet shamelessly, browsed my appearance, immediately, I recognised the person beside me.

He was my way into the Elites.

"No one who should concern you," I answered sweetly.

Instead of glaring, his smirk grew and there was this chilling flash in his grey eyes, his single sterling ear piercing glittering under the fluorescent light. I wanted to shift uncomfortably under his gaze – the old me would've — but in order to be like them, I had to remain strong otherwise I'd be like their other pawns that they played and got bored with. So, I steadily held his gaze, calculating my next move.

"Mysterious," he hummed in amusement. "I like it. Are you new then, mystery girl? I would've seen some as beautiful as you before if you weren't new."

I wanted to laugh. This was the famous Zane Stryker that Scarlett spent most her time talking about after realising that Bentley was never going to leave Celeste. I understood why everyone found him attractive; he was the stereotypical bad boy as Scar would describe him. Not only was he blessed, appearance wise, he had a charming personality and, from the five seconds I'd personally known him by, he was an incredible ass but apparently that was attractive to some people.

"I've honestly never met someone more attractive than Stryker, Candy," Scarlett sighed dreamily, triggering me to roll my eyes in nausea.

"I'm new," I responded as I directed my gaze elsewhere, the unnerving feeling of him staring me down and started to feel anxious.

What if he knew who I was? He couldn't have, Scarlett never talked about me to them —

"Are you not even going to give me a name? Even if I tell you that I'm Zane Stryker?"

I shook my head and fought back a smile when I saw him pout in frustration and irritation. He sighed and ran his fingers through his hair, squinting down where the rest of his friends were sitting, gossiping, scheming like the conniving weasels they were.

"How infuriating," he muttered more to himself than to me.

With one last fleeting glance at me, Zane Stryker strolled away, hands tucked into his pockets, and, without needing to say anything, I knew he was going to be back. I watched as he disappeared into the crowd before eyeing back towards the cafeteria instead.

The cafeteria was enormous, with a high ceiling and large tables neatly spread around the hall. In that current moment, it was filled with conversations about one another's summers and bubbling with laughter as groups of friends reunited. However, by some means, the hundreds of students were somehow subtly angled towards the middle table. That middle table consisted of seats for eight people which were fully occupied with the company of Harrington's Elites. Well, almost fully occupied. The eighth seat, which would usually house their past experiments or pawns, was empty today.

At one point, Scarlett had been the one sitting there.

It was scary to even imagine that she once associated herself with these people. My Scarlett wasn't manipulative, she was caring. She was loud and outgoing, but she would never act as if she was superior. Then again, maybe I didn't know her so well. One taste of the glitz and glam, and that's all it took for Scar to become Scarlett.

I always warned her to stay away from them, that they didn't have her best intentions at heart, but she was so stubborn and dead set on proving me wrong that she ended up having everything torn away from her. I wish she was here beside me so that I wouldn't be here to fend for myself, but she wasn't.

Bentley leaned down to whisper something to Celeste, which caused her to smirk in amusement. Her eyes flickered over to her left, quickly placing a smile on when the group of freshman girls noticed her stare. Whatever Bentley said next caused her to laugh which she quickly covered up with a cough. However, it was enough to know that the pair was talking about the freshmen.

The young girls burned with embarrassment and quickly gathered their things, rushing out of the cafeteria. Out of fear or embarrassment, it was difficult to say, but it did cause Bentley's smirk to widen and Celeste to giggle as she turned to him, gently kissing his cheek.

Even from the mezzanine, I could sense the amount of raw power and wealth that emitted off the group below, fuelling my hate and anger even more. They were entitled, they believed that everything and anything was theirs and did not care who they hurt. Their laughter was fake; it didn't take much to notice the tension between some members in the group from the way they tensed up to the way they'd look at each other. It was almost startling.

And in the centre of it all was Celeste Leon.

"You're all coming to the party this weekend?" Celeste questioned, but it sounded more like an order. At once, everyone agreed, and a satisfied Celeste leaned back in her chair with a triumphant smirk. They knew better than to refuse a party from the Queen herself.

By the end of the day, everyone knew about the upcoming party, a gathering to celebrate that everyone was back in the city, but, for the Elites, it was an excuse to find the next tortured soul to play with. Nevertheless, it was also the perfect time to make my presence officially known to them. So, for the rest of the week, I tried to remain invisible but, at the same time, gain a hint of their attention. I paid more care to how I looked, wearing red lipstick, straightening out my blonde hair, having my plaid red and black skirt cropped dangerously up my thigh, switching my flats to Louboutin's, which I wore above knee high socks, styling myself in the splitting image of a stereotypical popular girl.

I spent so much time assessing their lifestyle that it became so natural for me. The only way to take down your enemies was to become their friend and, if throwing out my glasses for contacts meant doing that, then I did it.

Even though, the anxiety gnawed against my stomach, scaring me into believing that this entire plan could fail, I already knew I was halfway there. Because, for the rest of the week at lunch, Zane Stryker would always glance in my direction.

I'm very excited.

Inspired by Clique Bait and Gossip Girl :)

You should check them out.

- fariha.

02 | pyramids

Chapter II: Pyramids

Hey Candy.

How could you think Celeste isn't beautiful? I mean her mother does own a major fashion magazine; she's natural born cover girl material. But I do agree with you. Once upon a time, I felt so privileged if Celeste even looked at me but now, she makes me want to run for the hills. I know it makes you upset that I damaged myself just to live up to her standards, but it was an addiction; being or even breathing the same air as they were like an addiction. Regarding your last question about who I am, I don't know the answer to that.

Please stay away from them, C. I don't want you to have the same fate as me. I don't want you to not know who you are. Hang out with the third clique; they are the only decent humans in that school.

I wish you never went in the first place.

Sent by Scarlett at 10:00 P.M.

***

SOCIAL HIERARCHY WAS said to be dated from over 7,000 years ago. The first case of it began with the Sumerians, religious people who belonged to the Mesopotamian civilization. The city expanded rapidly around the shrine of God, the increase of riches and wealth in food and resources creating a divide between their people.

Later, we have the Egyptians, who placed the Pharaoh at the top and the farmers and slaves at the bottom. To the Egyptians, the Pharaoh was God in human form; they believed he controlled their lives whilst they performed all the needful to make him happy.

You'd think that over a course of thousands of years, social hierarchy would be destroyed as people began to become more accepting over each other despite their wealth and family background but, sadly, that was never the case.

See, Harrington had a system, one that unlike a pyramid identical to the Egyptians. It was much more complicated and invisible, enforcing everyone into five categories, one Scarlett had put together during her time at Harrington. At the bottom were the freshmen, belittled by those above. There, not only would you find freshmen, but people who had been openly outcast by those in the higher cliques as punishment for overstepping their boundaries or challenging their authorities.

'Bottom feeders' were what people called them, people like Celeste. They were open targets, prey which could be easily hunted and suffered horribly. Above them, still following close behind, but far enough to at least have some amount of protection from the harassment, were the misfits. In simple terms, they were harmless and didn't fit in.

Then there was the safe zone, the third clique. It was a balance between in and out of being seen and not seen. Unlike the bottom two, the third cliques rarely faced any type of harassment from the higher groups, one could say because they were simply invisible. Scarlett called them 'Robin Hoods', at first I never understood why.

But one week at Harrington was all I needed to understand. The third clique were mostly artists, quiet and mellow students and the name was due to how they were simply the only group that had a sense of humanity. Although, they made minimal interactions with the lower cliques, they didn't disrespect them or made them feel inferior. The third clique just kept themselves to themselves; they weren't bothered by the other groups. They made Harrington seem normal, average.

Scarlett used to be them.

Until she got hungry for more.

Right above them, high enough that a fall could be drastically damaging to their social life, was the largest group in Harrington, consisting of people who wanted to be the Elites. They were the people who worshiped the ground people like Celeste Leon walked on, fuelling both the Elites' egos and power, a group residing of cheerleaders and jocks, even a few freshmen. They did anything from fulfilling tedious tasks to humiliate the groups below them just to gain the Elites' approval and attention.

Walking past a group of wannabes as I made my way to my table on the mezzanine, I meticulously observed them, trying to fathom how Scarlett became them. It was baffling yet hypnotising when I noticed that they were always on guard, ready for anything the Elites asked from them.

In fact, the moment Celeste Leon entered the cafeteria, hundreds of eyes staring at her arrival as if she was some sort of royalty. Two girls shot up from their table with a coffee and notebook at ready, rushing over to her side. Celeste didn't even acknowledge them, too busy with her conversation on the phone. Her green eyes narrowed into a frightening glare, causing a couple of people to look away submissively.

Finally, at the top of the social chain, our very own Elites. They were the highest you could get in Harrington. Everything and everyone revolved around them; they controlled not only the students, but the staff as well. Under their reign, the Elites had immense power that it was disgusting.

It horrified me that they had so much control and authority over everyone in the building. No one should have that much power. But with power comes scandals and, from what I had gathered, the Elites were the most scandalous clique in Harrington.

And I was going to become one of them.

How I was going to achieve that was something I had yet to figure out. Still, something told me it won't be long until an idea came to mind when I noticed Stryker sauntering over to me without that stupid smirk on his face, challenging eyes assessing me again, as if I was an object.

"To what do I owe the pleasure?" I demanded, sipping on my coffee.

Sliding into the seat opposite me on the table, he inclined forward, hands clutched together, a silver ring band on his ring finger, matching his earing. "Can't I say hi to my favourite mystery girl?"

Frowning, I shook my head, "Don't believe you."

That smug smile grew as he retorted back, "Didn't expect you to."

Momentarily, we held each other's gaze challengingly, on guard. Eventually, he leaned back into the seat, crossing his arms over his chest, briefly looking down at his friends below before focusing his startling grey eyes on me.

"Are you busy this weekend, mystery girl?" Zane asked with interest.

"Why?" I countered, narrowing my eyes tentatively.

"Be my date to Celeste's party. I have no doubt that you know what I am talking about since it's the latest hot news."

I scoffed, "Firstly, why would I agree to go with you? Secondly, who said I was even going?"

"Ah, don't be a Grinch," he joked, teasingly. "Think of it as your debut into Harrington. Everyone will be there; it could be the chance for you to branch out and meet new people to chill with instead of sitting up here alone for the rest of your Senior Year with me as your only friend."

Glaring, I replied defensively, "For your information, I quite like it up here. And who said you were my friend in the first place?"

Sighing, exasperatedly, he rose from his seat. "Just think about it."

Turning away from me, he began to walk down the stairs, greeting the jocks that sat on table not far from the Elites, their raucous clamour bringing attention to everyone in the cafeteria. Suddenly a light bulb went off and there it was: the idea that would get me into the Elites.

***

"Okay," I said when I strode past Zane in the corridors, heading into English. I didn't need to look behind me to know he was confused to what just went on because for a second, he didn't follow me but, when he finally did, he was by my side in a flash.

"Okay?" he questioned, incredulously. "As in okay, you'll be my date?"

I snorted, settling into my seat at the back on the classroom. "What else would I be saying okay to when it comes to you?"

Shrugging, he surprised me by taking the usually empty seat beside me, my eyes widening in genuine confusion and shock.

"Wh–What are you doing?" I hissed, astonished. With a smirk and a wink, he ignored me and my glaring eyes which were burning holes into the side of his face. When I noticed the teacher entering the room, I brought my voice level down a few notches as I whispered, "Can you please go back to your seat?"

Shaking his head, he sent me a sly grin, "Hush, I'm trying to listen."

Grumbling, I shuffled away from him slightly, a scowl evidently on my face, displaying my clear dislike, but it didn't faze him. Instead, Stryker made himself comfortable on the seat by leaning back, crossing his arms over his chest with that stupid, bloody, triumphant smirk on his face.

***

"How was school, sweetheart?" Mother asked as she entered the living room, my eyes flickering over to her away from my phone where I was researching into Celeste Leon.

Switching off my phone, I greeted her with a smile as she came and sat beside me, "Long and tiring. The students are unsurprisingly different to those back in London."

She snorted and rolled her eyes. "Trust me, my parents moving me to a boarding school in London was probably the best decision they made in my life. I don't understand why you were so adamant on attending a school in Manhattan, especially Harrington. Even after what happened with Scarlett."

"I just wanted a change of scenery and Scar told me so many great things about Harrington, I just wanted to experience it myself," I lied skilfully.

If my mother showed any signs of disbelief to what I was saying, she did a good job of not showing that. Mother sighed, leaning forward to place a soft kiss against my forehead before brushing away the stray strand of blonde hair dangling in front of my eye and tucking it behind my ear, gifting me her comforting motherly smile. These were rare moments I treasured since I barely saw her as she was always out the house.

"I just want you to be happy, Candace. Please talk to me if anything is wrong."

With a reassuring smile, I lied once more, "Of course. Anything."

Pleased with my reply, she gave my hand a small squeeze before leaving me alone, my thoughts haunting me along with my lies that I had no doubt would catch up with me one day.

***

I glanced at my reflection in the mirror on Saturday evening, assessing my outfit to see if it was suitable for a party at Celeste's. What did one wear to a party at Celeste Leon's? Muttering profanities under my breath, I shimmed out of the jeans and top, out of the clothes that made me feel safe and into something more daring, something that would catch their attention. A cute black dress that hugged my waist, enhancing my features, pairing it with a new set of Jimmy Choo's I had bought the other day.

Anxiously, I would check my phone every ten second to see if Zane had sent a message, informing me of his arrival, as I got ready. It still baffled me how he found my number. Honestly, it scared me when this unknown number popped up Friday evening, asking where I lived. At first, I contemplated calling it then blocking it until another message came up telling me it was Zane. Just as I coated red on my lips, my phone screen lit up with a new message from the devil himself, notifying me that he was waiting outside.

Gathering my things, I hurried downstairs, shouting out a rushed goodbye to my mother then heading out the house before she could question who was out there waiting for me. No need for any of the Elites to meet my mother, Zane included.

"Hey, stranger," he greeted with a grin from inside a gorgeous Bugatti, looking dashing in just a casual white shirt and black jeans. "You look beautiful."

I ignored the redness building on my cheeks and returned a smile as I settled into the seat beside him. "Thanks, you don't look to bad yourself."

"I feel very privileged to get a compliment from you," he teased as he shifted the gears to the car and set off to our destination. "Are you excited?"

"Define excited," I said, fighting back the anxiety that was threatening to reveal itself by distracting myself with the view of Manhattan's night life.

He chuckled, flashing me a side glance. "Don't be scared, we don't bite."

Oh, the irony.

Sending him a much more confident yet fake smile, I reminded myself of what the aim of going to this party was and to not stray from the task at hand because of Zane. "I'm not scared of anything, Stryker."

"Good because we've just arrived."

Celeste's home was astonishing and stunning. It was a large mansion that spread across more land than needed for a family of three. Lights from inside the house illuminated the outside, no need for streetlamps that pillared the road leading to the entrance of the mansion, on the opposite of the barred black gates.

Usually, these gates would be closed but tonight it was open, people in lavish outfits and cars flooding in and out. Zane parked up alongside the other expensive cars, my eyes not breaking away from the luxurious home. I, finally, snapped back into reality when the door opened and a hand was offered in front of me, breaking me out of my trance.

"Shall we?"

Slipping my hand into his, I smiled graciously as I stepped out of the car, setting foot onto the Leon's estate.

"This place is amazing," I whispered, voicing out my thoughts.

He laughed, probably amused by how awestruck I was. "I would hope so. Celeste's parents are extremely rich, nearly as rich as Bentley if I'm being honest."

That wasn't new information to me. Celeste's mother owned a world-selling fashion magazine and her father was a physician but, from my knowledge, he no longer lived with them due to difficulties with his marriage to her mother. Her parents split up when she was only 14. .

Clearly, all expensive ornaments were carefully hidden away as there were so many people; it was difficult to even walk through the crowd. Clutching onto Zane's hand so I wouldn't get lost, he led me through the sea of people, loud music blasting from the speakers along with chatter and laughter suffused the mansion. In the backyard was a large swimming pool filled with more people, squeals and screams as everyone enjoyed the pleasant evening weather.

"Where are you taking me?" I shouted to Zane so he could hear me over the sound of music and screaming.

He glanced back with a grin. "To meet new people."

At first, I frowned in confusion but then I noticed them, all sitting on couches underneath a gazebo that overlooked the yard, laughing and talking among themselves with unknown substances scattered across the glass table in the centre of them. Celeste was practically sitting on Bentley's lap as she rose a toast to all her friends, saying a few words before they all cheered and clinked their glasses of champagne against each other's, a wicked look crossing her face before she peered down to Bentley where he gifted her with a kiss.

"I don't think this is a good idea," I spoke out, bringing us to a halt.

"I thought you're not scared of anything," he retorted, causing me to give him a deadpan look. Exhaling, he took hold of both my hands, catching the attention of a few people, and looked at me with his grey eyes that startlingly reminded me of Scarlett.

"They'll love you," Zane assured with a soft smile, but I knew they wouldn't love me for the right reason.

Annoyed that I was going to have to start my plan sooner than I had hoped for, I sighed in defeat and nodded stiffly, causing him to grin victoriously before leading me up the stairs to the gazebo where the Elites sat. Almost immediately, their eyes shifted over to me with caution, their conversation and laughter cut short by my appearance besides their fellow member.

"Who's this pretty little thing, Zane?" Kato Takahashi questioned, an unfriendly leer crossing his lips as his brown eyes scoured me with interest.

"She has yet to tell me her name," Zane replied, glancing briefly at me.

Celeste's rosy lips curled in disfavour. "You don't even know her name and you brought her up here."

"It's a little game we're playing, Celeste. We all know how much you love games," he countered back sharply before sending me a wink. "Why don't you introduce yourself, mystery girl?"

Everything within me was telling me to run, run as far as I possibly could before I became their next pawn, their next victim to their wicked games. But I didn't. I had to do this for Scarlett and every other innocent person they tormented. I was going to take them down; I was going to break their chain and hierarchy. I was going to destroy the Elites. And with that, I sucked in a breath of air and mustered up a sweet smile, introducing myself to their world.

"Hi, I'm Candace."

-

I told my friends I'd post this on Wattpad.

I wonder if they've found me yet.

Hi *waves with a grin*

- fariha.

03 | mystery girl

C hapter III: Mystery Girl

Scar,

I don't understand how you sat beside them for so long, listening to all the disgusting things they say about people. Just being near them makes me want to run far away from them; they horrible people. How could such people exist?

The way Bentley looks at everyone is startling. It's like he knows exactly what you're feeling, or, even worse, thinking. His power over the people in Harrington is enormous, no one should have such control. Then, just this week, four freshmen dropped out of Harrington because Celeste and her cronies dumped yoghurt on them, started rumours, destroyed their reputation all because they didn't follow her rules. Her stupid, childish rules. How did you do it?

You'd never sit back a watch.

Sent by Candace at 12:00 P.M.

***

AT FIRST, NO ONE said anything. They just stared at me curiously, especially Bentley, who's eyes I'd rather not have caught. Noticing the sudden tension, Zane took hold of my hand, squeezing it comfortingly as he led us over to an empty couch, but this action specifically caught Celeste's attention, her jade eyes narrowing into sharp daggers that could've place someone six feet under.

"Candace," Celeste said wearily, my name sounding like it was filth in her mouth. "Did you recently move to Manhattan?"

"Yes. At the beginning of the summer with my mother," I responded, flickering my eyes vigilantly to all the other members who said nothing.

She hummed in reply, those cat-like eyes focusing primarily on me.

"I know you," Madeline suddenly blurted out with wide blue eyes, my heart stopping fearfully, and I held my breath. "I gave you a tour on the first day back. No wonder you sounded familiar."

I chuckled nervously, exhaling shakily, as she grinned at me, trying to calm my heart but at the back of my mind, all the warning signs rang furiously, telling me to leave now and not come back. I was scared, not matter how much I tried to deny it, just being near them made me hyperaware of everything occurring.

They seemed unaffected by my presence but, even then, I didn't want to give them a reason to think that I was hiding anything. They were all too weary of strangers, too suspicious of everyone and that's how their secrets were carefully protected and hidden from the public's eye. I couldn't be reckless, not even for a brief second.

"Do you want a drink?" Zane murmured, his lips brushing against my ear.

I tensed up, wordlessly nodding, which only caused him to smirk as he grabbed two empty glasses and poured some sort of yellow champagne. I didn't have any reassurance that it was something good, especially with white content messily sprinkled across the glass table.

None of the Elites were bothered about the fact that I knew some of them were doing drugs, like they knew I wouldn't say anything or maybe they knew how to make sure I couldn't say anything. The tension was thick, so suffocating that I forgot there were other people in yard as well. Thankfully, Zane broke the tension by initiating a conversation with Bentley.

"I heard your Dad is back in town. I thought he wouldn't be back until Christmas?"

Bentley shifted his focus away from me and onto his best friend, replying in a low tone which triggered shivers up my spine, "I thought so as well but it seems as if he has business here."

"Is he staying?"

The heir of the Harrington Industries shook his head, unbothered by his father's short visit. "It's a temporary stop over, and I wouldn't expect anything less."

Although, he seemed indifferent about the lack of visits from his father, there was an underlying iciness in his words. It was unsettling but everyone appeared to look unaffected. Celeste didn't even bat an eye, pouring herself and Bentley another glass of champagne. It made me wonder how often these people spent time with their family; it was like they were immune to anything sentimental.

"What else could we expect from him?" Zane snorted, which caused Bentley to smirk.

Soon after, the other's joined the conversation and the tension dispersed as they relaxed, quickly forgetting that I was even there. It gave me time to assess the members clearly since I finally could see them up close, and not from a far distance like where I sat on the mezzanine or behind my laptop screen.

There was Elijah Astor, a tech genius. He could find out information in a matter of seconds and although he was quiet, to Celeste, he was an important asset to the Elites. His strawberry blonde hair was tousled back, and there was this alarming glint to his hazel eyes when I noticed him looking at me.

I sent him a smile, but he didn't return one back, glancing away when Bentley said his name. There was something about him that made me uncomfortable, a guy like him had to have skeletons in his closet, too many in fact. It was only matter of time until they came out.

Madeline sat closely by Celeste, laughing at something that was said, her innocent blue eyes intoxicated by the alcohol. The two have been friends for God know how long, although, there was this period during junior year where Madeline went off the grid suspiciously out of nowhere, for reasons I was soon going to find out.

Madeline had every paparazzi on her wherever she went, she craved the attention and devotion that the public fed her, so it was puzzling why there was not a single article on her during that time. Celeste leaned down, murmuring something into Bentley's ear which caused him to tense up, but his facial expression made no change, expect the look in his eyes as he glanced up at her.

No matter how much I hated the pair, the way they looked at each other was intimidating and desirous; there was this aura of raw passion and dominance that I found it difficult to tear my eyes away. Caught up in their interaction, I must've not heard what Zane said because I felt him squeeze my hand, directing my attention to him.

"Sorry, did you say something?" I asked.

He frowned. "I just asked if you're okay. You zoned out."

I smiled reassuringly. "I'm okay. It just, you guys must be pretty close."

"Well, we have known each other since we were in Kindergarten," Madeline answered, surprisingly. "Expect the twins. Akari and Kaito met us in sixth grade. That literally feels like it was decades ago when we first met them."

Kaito snorted, pushing his silver hair back with his hand. "A reminder about that last time I saw my father."

Clearly, his twin sister didn't like that comment and shot him a scowl. "Shut up, Kai."

From what Scar had told me and further research, the Takahashi twins were brought up in Japan but moved to Manhattan when they were twelve, the same time their father's record label expanded on a global scale. They haven't seen him since.

"It's sad, you know," Scar whispered as we laid out on her yard, the stars being our only source of light. "I couldn't imagine the thought of not seeing my parents for so long, no wonder Kaito acts out. He just wants his dad's attention. Sometimes, I wonder if Akari knows that their dad isn't going to come back anytime soon. I think Kaito lies to her just so she doesn't get hurt, he's really protective over her."

"Doubt it," I muttered under my breath, the topic of the Elites really irritating me, but she was so fascinated in them, that I didn't have the heart to tell her that I no longer wanted to talk about these awful people.

"He wasn't always like that, C," Scarlett argued defensively after I made an insensitive comment about him, obviously upsetting her. "He used to be sweet surprisingly. Everyone loved him; he was like a ray of sunshine. I guess when he met Celeste, he realised there's finer things in life when you were wealthy. That's probably how he got caught up with dealing drugs and having a network of spies."

Unlike her brother, Akari was an aspiring singer, brought into the music industry when her father gifted her own branch of the Lion Entertainment for her sixteenth birthday. It was probably a gift given out of guilt. She had her own fair share of connections; they ranged from upcoming artists to A-list celebrities. Whereas, Kaito knew people who'd either get you sent to jail or killed.

Kaito didn't respond to his sister, consuming his nth glass of alcohol before slamming it against the table, and pouring himself another one angrily. Akari just rolled her eyes, tucking a strand of loose mahogany hair behind her ear, her lips curling in disapproval towards her brother's behaviour.

"Apologies for my brother, Candace," When Akari spoke, her voice sounded as soft like velvet, but her eyes said otherwise as they glowered at her twin in annoyance. "Father is a sensitive topic to him."

:Get over yourself, Akari," Kaito snapped, irately scowling at her, and soon they were both throwing dagger-like looks to each other, the tension building up between them. Until, a husky chuckle reverberated in amusement, breaking the glaring battle between the twins.

"Settle down, you two. You're going to scare our guest," Bentley teased, his haunting brown eyes focusing unnervingly on me.

As if she suddenly remembered my existence, Celeste frowned. "Who cares if she gets scared?"

"Celeste," Zane said warningly, his low tone shocking me, and as he glared at her, his hold on my hand tightened. Celeste could've retaliated at the way Zane showed her disrespect, she had the power too, but she didn't. Instead she sighed in exasperation and rolled her eyes.

"Fine. Have fun with your new toy."

"Oh, I think he will," Bentley smirked chillingly, fixating his attention on me meticulously as if he was daring me, challenging me, and I had no doubt that he wasn't.

***

That following Monday, I quickly gathered my belongings from my locker, rushing to English when the second bell went, indicating to me that I was now late. I huffed heavily, trying to catch my breath, before I entered the classroom sneakily. Successfully, I managed to slip into my seat besides Zane without getting caught by our teacher but Zane, on the other hand, shot me an amused look when he noticed how flustered I was.

"Why is Miss Prim–and–Proper late?" he whispered.

"The town car wasn't here this morning, neither was my mother," I answered with a frown to myself, my thoughts wondering to ideas on where my mother was all of last night.

"So how did you get here then?"

I shook my head, remembering the horrors of having to use a taxi. "I don't even want to think about it."

He snickered. "Must've been bad."

"You don't even know the half of it," I sighed, running my fingers through my hair, noticing the sheets in front of him. "What did I miss?"

"Not much," he replied, sliding a worksheet to me. "I was able to get you a spare, but you want to start acting as if you found your precious pen."

I frowned in confusion, furrowing my eyes. "I'm sorry, my what—"

Suddenly, interrupting what I was saying, Mr Andrew questioned, suspiciously, "Miss Lowell, did you find your grandfather's pen?"

My eyes widened for a second, Zane once again entertained, before I veered to Mr Andrew, fully composed with a smile. As I was about to reply, I noticed a silver pen above my worksheet that didn't belong to me but without a second thought, I picked it up to show my teacher.

"Right here."

His narrowed eyes didn't waver for a second before he sighed, relaxing the tensed features on his face. "Very well. Mr Stryker will inform you of what you have missed so far."

I smiled until Mr Andrew faced the board back again, continuing his lesson, before glaring at Zane, who was fighting back a laugh, his grey eyes twinkling in delight.

"I hate you."

"No, you don't, Miss Lowell," he winked before shifting his gaze back onto the board. "No one hates Zane Stryker."

I do.

-

What do you think of our characters so far?

Who do you hate? Who do you love?

- fariha.

04 | democracy

C hapter IV: Democracy

Candace,

I'm disappointed at myself. Not only did I let you down, I let myself down. But what could I have done? I was utterly terrified of her. She had the world in the palm of her hands, and she could crush mine without a second thought.

I wish I could take back everything I had done wrong; I wish so badly I could reverse time back to when it was just us in London. I can't. That's why I'm telling you to stay away from them, C, before you are forced to make the same mistakes I made. They won't change, no matter what you do, they will always be more powerful, and you won't stand a chance against them.

I love you, Candy. A lot.

Sent by Scarlett at 4:00 P.M.

***

BETWEEN LESSONS we usually get a short break so during one of them, I decided to head into the ladies' room to touch up on my makeup and tidy up my hair. Harrington never failed to impress because even the bathrooms looked a million dollars, with large mirrors on the walls, spotlights above them, a couch in front of the window and black-gold cubicles. Truly amazing the amount of money spent on the private school. Whilst I was in one of the cubicles, the doors opened and two sets of heels clicked against the marble flooring, along with their sweet yet frosty voices.

"Have you spoken to Bentley?" Madeline asked.

Celeste scoffed, "No, of course not. I wouldn't want to give him the satisfaction that he won the argument."

"It's been days since you last spoken to him properly," Madeline reminded. "Someone is going to notice something is wrong soon enough."

"Don't doubt me, Maddie. I know what I'm doing," Celeste snapped.

"I do not doubt you, Celeste. That's the last thing I'd do. I'm merely reminding you of the possibilities," Madeline said, firmly.

"I don't want reminders," Celeste muttered. "Did you get the photo and videos of Akari?"

"Of course," Madeline answered immediately. "She looks like a wreck. How is she ever going to be a singer?"

Celeste laughed; I could almost imagine a twisted smirk on her face.

"She won't, not if I have anything to do with it. That bitch is going to get what she deserves."

:So, what should we do with it?"

"For now, keep it hidden and when the time is right," Celeste ordered. "We'll use it to play her right into our hands."

Madeline snickered and without another word, the two left. I unsteadily exhaled, leaving the cubicle, trying to sort out my thoughts. Why did they hate Akari? It didn't make sense but, then again, with the Elites it never made sense. They did malicious things without reason, but something tells me the situation with Akari is much deeper than a petty argument, and I was going to get to the bottom of it. Washing my hands before fixing up my makeup and hair, I cautiously left the ladies room, checking to see the pair was around, before heading to my next lesson.

At lunch, Zane insisted on me sitting with the Elites and, despite my excuses, he eventually convinced (more like forced) me to sit with him. Instantly, every pair of eyes focused on me, the new girl, as I walked besides a confident Zane, who drank in the attention, as we walked towards the centre table. The Elites immediately quietened down when they noticed my presence, directing their attention onto me.

"And what is this?" Celeste sneered, her judgemental eyes glaring at me.

Zane smirked. "Candace, my date to your party. Surely, your memory is not that bad, Celeste."

"I tend to not remember irrelevant information," she scowled.

"Pity. Candace is anything but irrelevant."

"Don't irritate me, Zane," Celeste warned darkly, causing him to playfully put his hands up in surrender, fighting back a smile as he tried to maintain a serious look.

"Chill, Leon," he chuckled. "The table has been dead lately."

"I wonder why," Elijah muttered, looking away from us with furrowed eyes.

Ignoring his comment, Zane continued, "Candace is a breath of fresh air. I ensure it will benefit us all."

Far from it, I muttered in my head.

For a moment, no one said anything, possibly weighing out the pros and cons of having an extra addition to the table, a stranger. Maybe they also were trying to figure out how useful I could be to them. A new pawn, I could be their new challenge, their new entertainment. I could almost see the different types of methods they'd use to corrupt me, ruin me as they experiment new games. Perhaps, that's why Bentley spoke first.

"Well, we shouldn't be rude," Bentley's eyes were anything but friendly. They held intentions that were as menacing as his soul. "Take a seat, Miss Lowell."

Celeste may have hated the fact that I now housed the empty eighth seat, but she would never speak against her boyfriend's decision. Her cat eyes glared holes into my head before Bentley directed her attention elsewhere, squeezing her hand more tightly than necessary. If anyone else noticed that, they didn't say. Fully seated beside Zane, yet incredibly on edge, I began to eat whilst listening into their conversation, realising how eerily quiet the cafeteria had become.

As if reading my thoughts, Zane grumbled, "Bentley, do you mind?"

His best friend smiled darkly, and with a sharp glare directed to the groups below him, everyone fell back into their conversations as if nothing had occurred.

"Anyways, as I was saying, Mom is dead set on me going to Columbia since that's where she went but I have no intention of going there," Madeline groaned in irritation. "How comes Bentley gets to choose whether he wants to go to a college or not? It's unfair!"

"You seem to forget, sister, that I'm the heir to Harrington Industries. My role will become more crucial as Father steps down. I don't need college to prove myself unlike you, who's never committed to anything for more than a week," Bentley replied, nonchalantly.

"Don't start, Bentley," Madeline hissed. "You're pushing your luck."

The infamous smirk returned, his brown eyes twinkled in amusement, "I apologise, Madeline."

"Leave her alone, Bentley," Celeste sighed. "We have more pressing matters than you two bickering. Madeline, don't listen to your mother. If you don't want to go Columbia, then don't, but legacy is important, especially to your mother. Anything else?"

Madeline shook her head, unsatisfied, but Celeste didn't care and directed her attention to everyone else, ignoring her best friend sulking. It was like a democracy; Celeste was the leader and everyone else merely followed her command. Each of them expressed a concerned and, even if she didn't have a solution, she still gave advice which sounded more like orders. The issues they had were very minor and petty but, to them, it was like the entire world was falling apart and only Celeste could fix it.

"You're very quiet, Candace," whispered Kaito, who was sitting beside me. "Have nothing to say?"

I smile politely, "None. I prefer solving issues by myself."

He leered, leaning away with a glint in his eyes similar to Bentley's, "Of course, a clever choice indeed. One's secret cannot be used against them if it was never revealed in the first place. It's admirable."

Confused, I said questioningly, "Thank you?"

"You're welcome, Candace."

For a good minute, he continued to stare at me, probably trying to figure out my flaws, before Akari grabbed his attention instead. The twins secretly whispered to each other, everyone looking indifferent to their actions, almost as if this was a normal situation.

"Don't worry about Kaito," Zane murmured to me. Although he was speaking to me, his eyes were narrowed and focused on the silver-haired boy. "He likes to tease."

"I figured," I muttered, causing a crack of a smile from Zane as he moved his gaze onto me.

"I think you're going to fit in perfectly," he assured confidently, grey eyes bright with glee.

He was trying to comfort me because he assumed I was nervous about the fact that I wouldn't gain their approval, but he was far from the right answer. Fooling them was the easiest part, now I had to get at least one of them to trust me enough that they'd reveal the truth behind their lifestyles and spills secrets about the others.

However, every second I spent with them, I kept wondering if the cost would outweigh the benefits. How far would I have to go before they trusted me more than they had trusted Scarlett? How far would I have to change just to be like them, for me then to spin around and go against them? There were too many questions that I couldn't answer, but so many answers that I didn't want to question. I couldn't.

Not if I wanted to leave alive.

-

Bentley is by far my favourite antagonist I've created.

- fariha.

Chapter V: Daredevil

Regarding Bentley... Bentley is a very dangerous person, worse than Celeste. I couldn't even keep track on how many people he ruined during my time at Harrington.

See, the difference between Celeste and Bentley is that Celeste is impulsive. If a situation arises and she has information that could destroy someone in a matter of seconds, she'll use it. Whereas Bentley waits for the right opportunity. He patiently seeks out the right time to use what he has, and it has a permanent effect, more damaging than Celeste's. He keeps her grounded, you know.

Without him, Celeste would be nothing. She'd be defenceless.

Sent by Scarlett at 4:10 P.M.

****

SO WHY DIDN'T SHE destroy Akari then and there? The sudden thought came to mind as I was completing the work I had gotten set today. Setting my pen on the desk and turning my focus to my laptop, I quickly scrolled through Madeline's Instagram as she was the most active between the three of them. In a couple of minutes, on my bright screen was a picture of Celeste, Madeline and Akari during Spring Break.

It was just a picture, but pictures spoke a thousand words, louder than what occurred in reality. The three looked extremely close in this certain picture, drenched in water from head to toe, cocktails in their hands as they laughed together. The laugh wasn't forced unlike their next picture in the late summer, where they were gathered at someone's party.

The difference between the two was that in the latter, Akari looked extremely uncomfortable, a noticeably distance between her and the other girls. It was like she was shunned but as far as everyone was concerned, they were all still best friends. Leaning back against my chair, I sighed in frustration as I tried to rack up different scenarios but came to a blank. Suddenly, my phone lit up, Zane's name blinking on my screen as the phone rang until I picked up.

"Hey," I said, scrolling through Madeline's Instagram, smiling at the drunken photo of Zane that came up.

"Good evening, my lady," he replied. "Are you busy?"

Frowning, I answered, "No—"

"Great!" he interrupted enthusiastically, cutting me off before I could ask why. "I'm picking you up in 10. Be ready."

"Wait, wha—" I stared at my phone blankly when the phone cut off suddenly.

Groaning, I quickly changed out of the comfort of my joggers and into jeans, cleaning my appearance up before throwing a leather Mulberry coat over my top just as he arrived, honking the car horn plenty enough times to gain me complains from the neighbours' tomorrow. I cursed him under my breath as I slipped into my boots and left the house, the cold city air biting against my fingertips.

"You do know people are asleep?" I grumbled irately as I got into the car, but he didn't look the slightest bit concerned. What else was expected of him?

"You look nice," he complimented, ignoring my remark as he sped off before I could even put my belt on.

"Want to tell me where we are going?"

"Kaito is holding a small gathering," Zane answered. "Thought you'd want to go instead of doing nothing at home."

"Who said I was doing nothing?" I retorted, smartly.

He gave me a funny look. "You did."

"Shut up," I muttered, crossing my arms over my chest and staring out the window when I felt my cheeks heat up.

Chuckling, he said, "It's only a few people so don't worry."

***

"I thought you said there were only a few people," I said with wide eyes.

"This is a few," he answered with furrowed brows and a look of confusion on his face when he saw the horror on my face.

"A houseful is not a few, Zane!" I exclaimed, flabbergasted.

"Potato, patato," Disinterested, he strode towards the house with his hands in his pockets, causally greeting the people who walked past him.

With an irritated shake of my head, I sighed and walked to the very large estate. It wasn't as big as Celeste's but bigger than an average home in New York. It didn't have a street to itself, but largely took up the space, illuminated with numerous types of lights and decorated like a traditional Japanese house with a hint of modernity. The loud sound of people and music racketed throughout the entire street, no doubt disturbing their neighbours.

Becoming so distracted with my surroundings, I nearly lost Zane in the crowd of unfamiliar faces, so I quickly rushed over to him, tugging on his jacket to gain his attention. When he noticed it was me, a smile crossed his face before he led us upstairs to a private room with the rest of the Elites. It looked like another living room with its leather couches and glass table, a cherry blossom tree dominating a corner of the room with its mesmerising pink petals, the scent of alcohol in the air.

"Finally, you guys have arrived," Madeline said when she noticed us, before directing us over to where the rest of them where sitting. "We've been waiting for you. We were just about to play a game."

As usual, Celeste and Bentley sat beside each other, the others in their fixed seats as if they were invisibly reinforced onto them. Celeste disinterestedly looked at me halfway during her conversation with her other half, who had caused her to stop speaking when he saw me enter the room. There was this sudden flash of jealousy in her eyes and she hissed something under her breath to Bentley, inaudible to everyone else in the room, but it did catch his attention as he kissed her a moment after, murmuring something in return. Then there it was again. The aura of raw dominance between the couple.

"What game?" I asked, thanking Akari when she gave me something to drink, suddenly feeling parched due to the nervousness.

"A little spin the bottle," Akari replied with a friendly smile.

"Ever played it before?" Zane wondered.

"Only a couple of times."

"Good, then you know the basic rules. If the bottle lands on you, you either answer a truth or do a dare," Madeline instructed, placing a bottle in the middle of the table before spinning it. Anxiously, I watched it spin multiple of times before it slowed down, landing onto Kaito. He looked unbothered as Madeline grinned at him, excitedly.

"Truth or dare?"

Without hesitation, he answered, "Truth."

Before Madeline could give him a question, Akari quickly interfered, "Where were you last night?"

"I'm not answering that; I choose dare instead," he grumbled with a scowl towards his sister.

"Fine," Akari crossed her arms over chest and sent him a smug smile. "I dare you to tell us where you were last night."

Ignoring her, he turned to Madeline, "Well?"

She shrugged with a mischievous grin. "She gave you a dare. You can't cheat the system, Kai."

Kaito shot her a glare with his dark brown eyes before growling in frustration, answering so quickly that we almost didn't hear it, "With some girl."

For some reason, that must've been abnormal for the group to hear because even Bentley raised a brow in surprise. Guess he didn't know everything. A blush rose on Kaito's cheeks and before anyone could interrogate him; he spun the bottle which shifted the focus on Celeste.

"Dare," she said.

Madeline's grin only widened. "I dare you to kiss someone other than Bentley."

Celeste didn't look every slightly surprised or bothered and, without hesitation, stood up, striding to (what it seemed) Zane. However, shockingly, she surprised me by turning to Madeline at the last minute and planting a kiss against her best friend's lips. She didn't return back to seat until she shot me a confident smirk, knowingly playing mind games with me.

Madeline scowled playfully at Celeste, who shot her wink as everyone laughed. "It had to be me."

"Love you, Mads," she teased before spinning the bottle where it landed on Akari, suddenly causing the vibrant ambiance to turn into tension as the Japanese girl looked marginally worried when Celeste stared at her, emotionlessly but still filled with meaning. "Truth or dare, Akari?"

She did a very good job of hiding the fact that she was actually nervous and smiled confidently at the brunette. "Truth."

Celeste smirked, leaning back into Bentley's arm that rested around her shoulders. To everyone else, it must look like she was about to tease Akari as friendly banter because that was the norm, but I knew otherwise. The look in her jade eyes said otherwise; it was cold and calculating, it was devising her next move in this game and her final win.

"Have you ever slept with anyone...." she paused, letting the words settle over Akari. "Within the group?"

Without blinking, she returned a smirk. "Yes."

From the corner of my eyes, I notice Zane frowning in puzzlement at Akari's answer, his grey eyes crinkled up when he creased his brows. He opened his mouth to speak but I gently touched his hand, seizing his attention. Glancing at me, I shook my head softly and watched him understand my message before downing another drink. However, Kaito on the other hand, had a murderous look in his eyes which Akari quickly silence with a glimpse his way.

Celeste, discontented with her answer, hummed as a reply before spinning the bottle. Bentley callously stared down at his girlfriend, who sat with a dull expression on her face, and squeezed her shoulder, directing her attention to him. No one paid attention to the pair as the bottle landed on Madeline, who enthusiastically grinned as she asked for a truth, but I did. To the smallest of details.

He seemed upset with her - no, he was disappointed, irritated. Celeste didn't waver as she fiercely glared, clenching her jaw and the hold on her glass of alcohol; I think I heard glass crack. Bentley sighed, getting rid of his arm around her and removed any other types of emotions before standing up, bringing out what looked like a joint.

"Shall we leave the girls for a bit?" he asked, directing the question to the boys, who all grumbled out a reply as they got up from their seats and followed Harrington out of the room.

Celeste drawled, leaning back into the seat, "Well, this is boring."

"Not at all," Madeline answered with a frown, her blue eyes once again intoxicated. "We can have girl time. Maybe Candace can spill about Zane and her."

Wide eyes with shock, I laughed in embarrassment. "Nothing is going on."

Akari rolled her eyes. "Oh, please, Candace. Zane never takes this amount of interest in a girl. Usually they don't even last through a day."

"So, what makes you special?" Celeste grilled, that familiar look in her eyes told me she was fishing for information, it told me to play the game carefully or I'll be caught by the hook too early.

"I don't know," I shrugged with a small smile. "It's a mystery to me."

"A mystery indeed," Celeste said carefully then a smirk grew on her face, slowly. "But all mysteries unravel in the end. Don't they, Candace?"

There was so much meaning held in her words, so much power that could break down my barriers, but that just meant I had to be smarter, tougher and quicker than her. However, what became my latest concern was how far she was willing to go in order to, not just, discover my secrets, but destroy me as well because from the little scene created between her and Akari, it seemed that she didn't care about anyone she ruined.

She was ruthless.

People could argue that Bentley was worse but as she sat opposite me, sipping on her glass with her stupid, snarky smirk and twinkling cat eyes that studied me as if she was memorising my every action, waiting for me to slip up; I questioned otherwise. One mistake from me meant my grave in the society. So, I steadily held her gaze as I lifted my glass with smile.

"They all do."

-

Mysteries are always a bunch of fun.

- fariha.

06 | symphony

C hapter VI: Symphony

Scar,

Akari and Celeste don't seem to be on the same page. But Celeste still wants to control her every move. Just the other day, I was speaking to Akari, having a normal conversation and Celeste hated that. I heard the pair arguing during lunch; they didn't notice me, and I couldn't fully make out their conversation, but I definitely heard my name along with some colourful words afterwards.

Akari is sweet and seems so genuine but when I remember what she did to you, it reminds me that it's just a façade, nothing but a little act she's putting up and fooling the people around her. Although Madeline is the high school sweetheart, at least she doesn't lie to your face about who she likes. Akari, on the other hand, is too perfect. Like a painting. And I hate it.

Sent by Candace at 12:00 A.M.

***

AKARI DIDN'T JUST sound like a popstar, she looked exactly like one. Her sense of style was wealthy with a side of playful; she was sophisticated but being in the room with her brightened the entire atmosphere. She was beautiful with her long, mahogany hair that reached her waist and brown eyes that looked gold in the sunlight. She suited every outfit she wore; from jeans to dresses, regardless of colour. She reminded me of a painting, delicate yet worth millions.

At least that's what I told her.

"Really?" she blushed, tucking a strand of loose hair behind her ear as we walked to class together. "You flatter me, Candace."

"I'm serious, Akari," I grinned.

"That's really sweet of you. I haven't heard a compliment so genuine before, it just seems weird," she laughed but it was pained slightly.

I frowned as we entered the classroom, loud chatter filling the room. "Really? Do your friends not compliment you?"

She shrugged, smiling feebly. "I guess but they aren't... You know."

"Yeah, I do," I sighed, feeling sorry for her.

"Hey, don't get too hung up on it," she consoled, shoving me softly with a grin when she noticed the sombre look on my face. "How about I sit with you today? Celeste isn't in a good mood today and I don't really want to deal with her."

"Are you sure?" I asked carefully as we walked to my desk at the back.

"Yes. Don't worry, she won't care," Akari answered with a laugh.

But she did. Even if Celeste wasn't on good terms with Akari, she did care where her friend sat. Especially, if it was with me. I could feel those green eyes throwing daggers our way, my way. I refused to look in her direction, not matter how tempting it was and focused on the bubbly Japanese girl who sat beside me, the diamond pin in her hair sparkling under the incandescent sunlight.

"Tell me about your singing. Do you write your songs? Have you recorded before?" I wondered. Suddenly, her eyes lit up joyfully and she grinned like a little kid.

"I wrote a couple and recorded them too, I'm just trying to find my sound, but I can't, and it's been really hard lately, especially with my brother and everything else."

"So, you haven't had time to sit down and just relax?"

She shook her head, letting out a little sigh before placing that smile on her face again which I couldn't tell if it was real or fake because her shoulder slouched as if she was holding so much weight.

"But we have a Japanese saying, 'Wake from death and return to life,'" she stated. "It just means to turn a bad situation into success. Father used always remind me that when I was younger."

"You and your dad are pretty close," I pondered and this time, I knew that smile was genuine because it reached her eyes, her dimples revealing themselves.

"We are. After our mother passed away, when Kaito and I were just babies, Father literally turned everything around and completely changed. By the time we turned twelve, Lion Entertainment was on a global scale, named famously after the nickname my father gave my mother," Her eyes turned sad, but she smiled faintly at the memories, the reminders of the past. "Mother had the most stunning red hair in the sunlight, although her hair was naturally brown, she had this tint of red in the sunlight which many found strange, but father was absolutely in love with it, with her. I think he secretly wished I inherited that trait from her sometimes."

After a moment or two, I quietly whispered, "What was her name?"

Akari didn't speak for a second; she silently stared ahead for the longest minute before glancing at me, smiling with unshed tears glittering in her coffee-coloured eyes. "Eri."

*

The situation between Akari and her friends must've been much worse than it looked because it didn't take long for her to trust me easily, spilling every worry and thoughts in her pretty little head, forgetting my position in the group. Instead of heading to a café, which she'd usually attended with Celeste and Madeline every Monday for the last 5 years, she invited me to visit the Lion Entertainment branch situated in Manhattan. This branch was under her name and although she owned it, she had other people monitor it for her whilst she finished her education.

"And here's the recording studio," she said, switching the lights on to the room. "I spend most of my time here nowadays."

"Whoa," I whispered as I took in the room with a booth and professional equipment used to record. I noticed the plaques on the wall, awards for Mr Takahashi and some of the artists belonging to the company. "This is amazing."

"It is something, isn't it?" she grinned.

"Can you show me one of your works?" I asked hopefully.

She hesitated, "I don't know."

"It's okay if you don't want to, I'm just curious," Smiling encouragingly at her, she eventually gave in with a sigh, quickly setting up the computer.

"When I give you a thumb up, just press the play button," she instructed.

"Yes, ma'am," I said, beaming.

Akari rolled her eyes before shuffling into the recording booth, placing the headphones on and getting herself ready and comfortable. When she gave the thumb up, I pressed the play button on the computer and immediately after, a melodic tune vibrated out of the speakers and her voice followed soon after. She truly was amazing.

Her voice was perfect, soft and harmonic, easily reaching those high notes as if they were nothing. She made the song alive, her voice soulful and fresh, it was enchanting and mesmerising. Akari looked so peaceful as she sang, invested in the music, her eyes closed as she swayed, a small smile on her face.

For the longest second, she didn't look like she was part of the Elites; she didn't look like she could hurt someone so mercilessly. When she finally opened her eyes, a grin crossed her face as she effortlessly reached that final note. I was speechless and still speechless when she got out of the booth.

"Well? What do you think?" she questioned nervously when noticing that I haven't said anything. "Candace?"

I took a moment to collate my thoughts and grinned widely at her. "That was amazing. Akari, I haven't heard someone sing like that in so long."

She giggled, tucking a strand of hair behind her ear as she blushed in embarrassment. "That was nothing."

"Nonsense, that was talent," I said, persistently. Akari didn't say anything for a long period of time then a stunning yet genuine smile was painted cross her face. I could tell she wasn't used to the compliments; her friends must not give them to her enough.

"You're too nice, Candace," Akari said softly. "It doesn't seem real."

"It is real, Akari. You just don't get enough people telling you that you're amazing, so I don't blame you for questioning whether I'm being genuine or not," I shrugged. "Honestly, you have pure talent."

"Thank you, Candace," she replied, wearing a gentle expression on her face.

But I still saw the cracks. I knew I got to her. So, I took her hands in mine and smiled so widely that my cheeks began to hurt.

"Call me Candy."

*

Time went quickly whenever I was around the Elites. It was parties after parties, endless gatherings after gatherings when I was with them. Some days I forgot what my goal was, I'd curse myself because it meant that I was falling in their trap, their illusion. After a couple of weeks of being with them, the Elites began being less guarded, excluding Celeste, and were more relaxed whenever I was around, including me as if I was always one of their own.

Zane, being as infuriating as ever, would randomly take me to different places without warning, introducing me to the most beautiful locations in New York. When I was with him, I couldn't help but forget everything and focus mainly on him. During lunch, we'd spend most of our time talking to only each other or we'd eat someplace else, something Celeste highly disliked. She openly hated us being together.

"Won't she be mad?" I questioned, warily, as he took my hand, leading me to his car. "She said to meet her at that café."

"It's only for one day, Candace," he sighed, waiting for me to get inside, which I did (reluctantly if I may say so). "Let me handle her."

I didn't reply to him, sieving through my messages which consisted of Akari telling me about her and Celeste's latest argument. By spending more time with Akari, I realised that Celeste never really liked her, and I believe it was because of Bentley. Something Akari said was constantly on my mind, and it was bothersome, but I just couldn't put the pieces together. However, with Zane I have no doubt it would make sense.

"Hey, Zane," I began, getting a hum as a reply from him. "Were Akari and Bentley ever a thing?"

He snorted and shook his head. "God no. Celeste has had her claws in Bentley for as long as I can remember. Why do you ask?"

I shook my head dismissively. "Nothing. It's just I realised that Celeste hates it whenever Bentley talks to Akari or is even near him."

"Well, Akari and Bentley were really close when the twins first arrived at Harrington. It was kind of weird, but I think Akari understood him, in ways that I couldn't," Zane stated as he turned into a parking lot. "We're here."

"And what is here?" I asked as I unclipped my seatbelt, trees surrounding our environment as far as the eye could see.

Smirking, he replied mysteriously, "You got to wait and see."

I frowned as he led us through the carpark, carrying a picnic basket in one of his hand, before venturing deep into the forest which eventually led to me to conclude that he found out the truth and was about to murder me. The scary part was that he could get away with it and no one would blink an eye in his direction.

"Zane," I murmured, quietly. "I'm sorry."

He laughed. "I'm not going to kill you, Candace. Stop panicking."

Exactly what someone would say if they were about to kill me.

Eventually, there was this glimmer of light that broke through the canopy of trees, causing Zane to glance back with a tender smile on his face, which melted my heart as it made him look so innocent and serene; his typically harsh, grey eyes filled with mischief was now gleaming with warmth, specks of sapphire glittering in his eyes when the sunlight illuminated him.

"I come here when I want to get away from home, or even Celeste," he muttered as I became in awe with the beautiful lake that glimmered underneath the sun, flowers of all colours scattered around, and the grass was looking lush green; the entire view seemed ethereal.

"This place is absolutely stunning," I said in astonishment, leaning down to touch the water. "How did you find it?"

"It was so long ago, I actually can't remember," he chuckled, softly. "But since then, I've been coming here whenever I needed a break."

"So why did you bring me here?" I asked, suddenly realising that he placed a blanket on the grass whilst I was distracted by the scenery.

"To get away from our friends," he replied as he opened the basket. "Sit down."

When I finally sat down, he handed me a sandwich that cracked a smile from me, "You made these?"

"I can make food, you know," I bit back a laugh as he shot a playful glare in my direction. "I made most of this, Candace, so be prepared to be blown away with my master cooking skill."

I grinned at Zane, his eyes bright with enjoyment, "You're full of surprises, aren't you?"

He smirked, not answering my question, and took a bite in the sandwich. As we ate, the silence between us wasn't awkward; it was comfortable like we were embracing each other's presence. The weather was surprisingly warm, especially how we were close to December, but it made this entire afternoon even more memorable.

Zane lived very simply; it was something I noticed whilst spending time with him. He had his fast cars, lavish fashion brands and a humungous home, but, in actuality, he was very content with small things, like this place. It also made me feel bad that I was using him.

"Why are you staring?" Zane questioned, breaking me out of my trance. My cheeks burned with embarrassment as I ducked my head down, hair shielding me away from his scorching gaze.

"This sandwich is really good," I muttered, shyly, which gifted me his laughter.

"You're something, Lowell," he chuckled, my blush darkening when I finally had the courage to look in his direction, a wide grin painted across his face.

"How did you even become friends with them?" I blurted out, unexpectedly.

At first, he looked surprised, then hesitant before answering me, "I grew up with them, I guess that's all there really is to it."

I didn't know why that surprised me; of course, that was why he remained friends with them. The Elites were so tight knitted that it was impossible to tear them apart, they've watched each other through the good and bad times, and they know each other's darkest fear and worst secret. Although that seemed like a disadvantage for me, it wasn't. It made them easier to break. It was a weakness that left them vulnerable if one was to play their cards right. I certainly was going to be that person.

"They still make me uncomfortable," I said, truthfully.

"They still make me uncomfortable," he mumbled, my eyes curiously narrowing at him.

"What do you mean?"

"They're very..." Zane paused, his eyes flickering everywhere as he tried to gather the right word to use. "Different."

Different was definitely one way to describe them.

Noticing the way my eyebrow lifted up in surprise, he sighed. "They're a bit callous with other people. I just don't agree with it sometimes."

"You don't have to agree with them all the time, Zane. You're allowed to have your own opinions," I stated.

"Celeste doesn't see it like that. Her word has been, and will always be, final. Last time someone stood against her, it didn't end so pretty," he revealed, opening a tub of strawberries.

Could he be talking about — No, he couldn't.

"What happened to them?"

He didn't respond for the longest time and that was enough to confirm my suspicions. His eyes obscured as if he was remembering something, his jaw clenched, and his fists tightened. Instead of answering me, he shook off the dark look that crossed his face and sent me wink with a grin; the sudden change of persona shocking me.

"I'm going to go for a swim, want to join me?"

I smiled, shaking my head, "I'm good."

As he set off toward the lake, I sat there, breathing steadily and fighting away the tears from falling, reminding myself that he could've stopped them. But he didn't.

No one did.

-

Time will only tell whether she will succeed.

Or will she fall down the same road as everyone else?

- fariha.

07 | relics

C hapter VII: Relics

It's been a while; I'm sorry for not being in touch with you but spending time with Akari, and occasionally Zane, seemed to take a lot of my time. I've applied to the colleges I plan on going to after Harrington, but it seems to be the last thing on my mind. Celeste still doesn't like me and, only recently, Madeline acts indifferent when I'm around. Maybe it's because me and Akari have gotten closer. Since I've been around Akari, I've learnt so much about her and Kaito (who still makes me feel unsettled).

Kaito is messed up. I feel bad for Akari sometimes, not knowing all the things her brother gets up to. Her name could be ruined because of him; any chances of her being famous could be go down the drain if word got out about his business.

Maybe that could work to my advantage.

Sent by Candace 12:00 A.M.

***

KAITO, LEANED AGAINST his car, was talking to a pretty, blonde after school one day. Her hand resting on his bicep as she smiled flirtatiously at him, batting her false lashes at him when he whispered something. It was nauseating as I watched from the distance. She laughed at something he said, a smirk on his face as he studied her like she was a trophy. Moments later, the pair got into his car, backing out of the car park just as my town car pulled up in front of me.

"Follow that car," I ordered the second I got in. "But don't make it obvious."

The driver complied, staying steadily behind the Mercedes, the engine revving as it veered in and out of other cars. At one point we lost it but, surprisingly, my driver had no trouble catching up with them a few minutes later. Eventually, we ended up in Queens, the roads quieter than Manhattan, fewer cars on the roads, much fewer people outside. I frowned as the Mercedes turned into a driveway and, not far away; I observed them as my car came to halt a few blocks down the street.

"Stay here," I said, grabbing my things as I left the car, careful to not make any sound.

Kaito and his blonde friend walked up the stairs of the house, hands locked together as he knocked on the door only once before patiently waiting outside. As if he could sense someone watching him, he glimpsed in my direction, causing me to duck quickly behind a car, breathing heavily as my heartbeat increased due to the pressure.

When I felt I was in the clear, I peered out to the side to see the pair entering the home. It was unclear of who opened the door, I couldn't tell from this far which frustrated me as it meant going closer which, consequently, could blow my cover, but I took the chance and sneakily made my way to the house.

I pressed myself against the side of the house and steadied my breathing, cursing myself for being so unfit. I noticed an open window not far from where I was standing which was displaying the events occurring inside.

"Did you get what you wanted?" Someone said, a hoarse voice as if they had just woken up.

"Of course," I recognised Kaito's voice the second he spoke and could almost imagine his haunting smirk on his face. "Do you have the cash?"

"All thirty thousand packed in those bags just for you, Takahashi," Someone else replied, much softer than the other. "Do you want us to take it to the regular?"

Kaito didn't speak for a second, it was quiet, and I was itching to see what was going on inside, but I held back the temptation. I couldn't get caught, especially in the neighbourhood I was in, who knew what could happen to me?

"Yes, preferably in the next hour. Drop one of these off as well."

His word was final and, after a few minutes of shuffling about, the front doors opened, the car engine turned on before the sound faded into the distance as he sped away. I weighed out my chances of being caught if I peered through the windows before doing so. The room was crowded, not with people but boxes, stacks and stacks of boxes until it's was almost impossible to enter the room. Surprisingly, they all commonly shared the same word printed across box.

K.T.

It wasn't hard to realise that these were Kaito's initials, but what was difficult was to see what was within them. The boxes were all tightly secured, taped up with a small security sensor attached to the side. It was frustrating as that meant any chances of opening the boxes would cause the alarm to go off, exposing me to whoever was in the house. I had no doubt that Akari didn't know what was occurring in Queens, she never does when it comes to her brother, so asking her would only raise suspicions, more so if I asked anyone else in the group.

Therefore, I decided my only answer would come from following whoever left house next to drop off the cash and box. Cautiously, I head back to the car, glancing over my shoulder every five seconds in paranoia. As soon as I was in the safety of inside my car, I instructed my driver on what he was to do when I spotted two burly men, packing a Rover with bags of cash and a single box, before driving off. The Rover took us out of Queens, the roads getting busier as we soon entered Manhattan again.

The shift of location made me feel much more comfortable and less tense, the unsettling feeling gnawing against my heart disappearing. I don't know long the journey was but soon we pulled up a few cars behind them in front of what looked like a club. The burly men wasted no time in getting out and relocating the delivery into the building, which was flooding with people.

It was too obvious for me to enter in my uniform, anyone could notice me, so with a quick memorisation of the location, I asked to be sent home but not before messaging Akari about our plans tonight.

*

"Where are we?" She said with a surprised look on her face as we stood in front of the club with a blinking neon sign that illuminated the street, enhancing the Manhattan nightlife.

"I thought we could go clubbing and I heard a couple of girls talking about this place," I replied innocently then frowning when I saw her eyes flicker nervously. "If you don't want to be here, we can go someplace else."

"No," she answered instantaneously, as if she didn't want to offend me. "It's your first night club in Manhattan, we might as well check it out and see if it could be our regular."

I grinned at the Japanese girl who stood out in the crowd with her shimmery red dress and red bottom heels. She returned one back before placing her fingers with mine, dragging us towards the entrance. The bouncer asked for names and, although I didn't book us entrance, I knew the moment Akari said hers, we'd be let in immediately.

"Akari Takahashi and — "

The bouncer's expression changed and startlingly became less tense as he interrupted her, opening the doors. "Miss Takahashi."

Akari was surprised herself, looking at the men with confusion but didn't question it as we entered the club. I had a feeling this club had some sort of relation with the Takahashi's and this just confirmed my suspicious, a triumphant feeling bubbling within me.

Let's see what you're hiding, Kaito.

The ambience of the club was vibrant, speakers blasting music, crowds on the lower ground as strobe lights flickered wildly whilst on the platform was the bar and tables seating groups of all types. It was quite different to what I experienced in London, much more intense. Akari squealed in excitement and, without any warning, she dragged us towards the bar where she enthusiastically orders some sort of concoction for the both of us.

"Akari, how did that bouncer know who you were?" I questioned once we seated ourselves at an empty booth, sipping our drinks.

She shrugged. "Maybe Kaito is a regular. Clubs and places usually let me in because they know him, but it's weird that I haven't heard of this one."

"He won't say anything about us being here, right? I mean, he probably didn't tell you for a reason."

"I'll deal with him if he says anything, plus it's not like you knew," I nodded in agreement and she smiled. "Exactly. Just have fun, Candace."

"I trust you," I teased and Akari's rosy lips curved into a smirk.

"Well, you should trust me to get us a stronger drink," Before I could protest, she snatched my cup out my hand and sauntered over to the bar, catching a few people's attention along the way, eventually talking to a guy at the bar.

Taking this opportunity, I slipped out of the booth and wandered around to see anything out of place but there were so many people, it was difficult to get past them. Somehow, I found myself in a corridor which not only led to the lavatories but, further down, headed towards a closed door at the end of the corridor.

I hesitantly opened it, slipping into the room before anyone could see me. I was greeted with boxes, similar to the ones I saw this morning, the cash nowhere to be seen but that was the least of my concern as I noticed a box was opened. Briefly checking for any security cameras, remarkably not finding any, I inspected the box to see if the security sensor was active and when all was clear, I looked inside. Frowning, I pulled out the item hidden within the Styrofoam's.

"A vase?"

I wasn't sure I was expecting, maybe drugs given his reputation, but this was unexpected. It baffled me why he had a vase inside this box. Carefully, I returned it back in its original position when something else poked me, causing me to flinch in discomfort.

Naturally, I lifted that item out of the box, once again astounded to see a jade figurine of what looked like solider, but it was hard to tell due to the powder covering it. Suddenly, I could hear chatter and footsteps heading in this direction and panic rose within me. Calmly yet quickly, I snapped a picture of the two items before closing the box, ducking behind a stack of them in the corner just as the door opened.

"What did Boss say we do with them?"

"Transfer them to the warehouse. The move here was only to get the feds off our back. By the time we move them, they'll come to a dead end."

After a couple of sentences passed between them, they left, the door clicking behind them. Locking me in the room filled with contrabands.

*

I was panicking. My hands got all sweaty, my heart beat increased, my mouth got dry and I couldn't breathe. It felt like I was suffocating as if the oxygen levels dropped rapidly in the room. My subconscious was telling that there was no use of panicking, the longer I stayed in here then the chances of being found tripled. Every second I wasted not doing anything could be second closer to my cover being blown. Chanting that repetitively in my mind, eventually, the anxiety vanished, and it felt like I could breathe again. I stood out from behind the stacks of boxes, praying that my skills to pick a lock weren't rusty as I took out a bobby pin from my hair.

"Scarlett," I hissed as I watched her unlock her dad's office door with a bobby pin. "What are you doing?"

Nervously, I glanced down the corridor, afraid we would get caught, but Scarlett wasn't the slightest bit concerned as she sent me a mischievous grin. She had a twinkle in her eye filled with amusement when she saw the panicked look across my face.

"Stop fretting, C," she scolded before paying her attention back to the task at hand.

"Why are we doing this again?" I sighed, apprehensively.

"Because, my sweet Candy," she paused and suddenly I heard a click. I looked at her with disbelief as she beamed victoriously. "We are going to see where my darling father is sending me off after summer."

"I don't think—"

She interrupted me with a hush, silencing me with a sharp glare before opening the door. Unenthusiastically, I followed after her as she slipped into the room, switching the lights on and watching it illuminate the mahogany furniture, a couple of family portraits here and there, a wall-long bookshelf and a fireplace.

"Go search in those cabinets, I'll go check his desk," she ordered, leaving no space for any arguments.

I wasn't sure how long we spent looking, it felt like hours when it could've only been twenty minutes, but the more time I spent searching for these documents; the less I believed they were even in this room. I groaned as I closed yet another drawer, turning to my best friend and watching her wildly seeking the answers she so desperately wanted. I cringed when she growled in frustration, slamming the piles of paperwork onto her father's desk.

"Scar," I whispered, uneasily. "Maybe it's not here—"

"Aha!" Scarlett shouted, causing me to flinch. She beamed, grinning from ear to ear as she waved the documents in the air; she looked beautiful under the dim lights. "I told you. I'm always right, Candy. When will you learn that?"

The door unlocked successfully, and I wasted no time in leaving the room, locking the door and rushing back to Akari. Thankfully, she hadn't returned to the table, still distracted by the guy at the bar however, as if she could sense me staring, she glanced in my direction with an apologetic smile. Eventually, she left him; I could almost imagine him pleading her to stay just by the annoyance that crossed her facial expression. Although it was brief, it was there.

Clearly, he didn't notice that as his hand shot out to stop her from leaving. Her eyes flashed dangerously dark as they narrowed, her lips curving into a scowl when she leaned down, muttering something to him. The tension on his shoulder was visible when she shrugged his hand off her and sauntered back to our table.

I frowned and said, "Everything good?"

"Men are so entitled. They act sweet at first but the second you say no or reject any advances, they switch," she grunted. "It's outrageous."

"Don't let him ruin your mood," I said. "The night is still young."

She hummed, sipping on her drink and absently looking into the distance. There was a moment of silence before her eyes flickered back over to me, suspicion lingering within them as she asked, "Where did you disappear off to for so long?"

I stiffened. She's smarter than I thought.

"I went to the bathroom and then bumped into an old friend," I answered, innocently.

"Who? I thought all your friends are in England."

"They are but one was visiting her grandmother for the weekend, it was a coincident that we saw each other."

"Can I meet her? Is she still here?" Akari questioned, eagerly, with wide eyes filled with curiosity.

Shaking my head, she pouted in disappointment, but it didn't last very long when the change in music caused a change in her mood. Without any warming, she took my hand and dragged us to the ground floor, the look of perplexity covering my face.

Noticing this, she grinned. "Like you said, the night is still young, and this is my favourite song!"

I shook my head and laughed.

*

The night, after Akari dropped me home, I changed out of the sweaty dress and into something more comfortable before getting underneath my covers and pulling my laptop onto my lap, transferring the pictures from my phone. I made multiple copies, just in case, hidden in various types of files. I couldn't take the risk of losing the evidence.

I quickly had put the pieces together of what was inside those boxes after hearing the conversation between Kaito's men; he was smuggling relics and not just any type but cultural relics. They were definitely shipped from Japan, possibly China, however it was hard to determine whether they were genuine and if so, it would be enough to send him away for a very long time.

I smirked, amused by how well this was all working out. Some part of me felt bad that I was betraying them, guilty that I'm misusing their trust but the majority part of me wouldn't be satisfied until their name and everything they have was in the dirt. Scarlett wanted me to do this, so she could finally rest knowing that justice was served and that everything will be okay. So, she could finally be happy and in peace.

I wouldn't know that for sure until I succeed in what I had come to do. The main reason I came to Harington, the main reason I had befriended those malicious people. Everything I was doing; I was doing for her. I was here to finish what she had started.

By the time I was done with them, no one will ever bow to the Elites again.

-

What do you think of Akari?

- fariha.

08 | humiliation

Chapter VIII: Humiliation

Candy, I'm sorry that I haven't been messaging you. It's been a while, hasn't it?

Don't apologise, I don't blame you. The Elites have that way with people, they're enchanting, memorising and... I was once in your position, I ignored you. I now understand how you felt, I'm sorry. I wish I could take it all back, I wish... Anyways, don't worry about Maddie and Celeste, if one person doesn't like someone, the other won't as well. It's just how they work. And, Kaito has always been unsettling; that boy hasn't changed. He is smart, so be careful of him.

He has eyes and ears everywhere. As for his sister's future, it's unsure. Celeste has held a huge grudge against her for so long that this dream that Akari holds seems to be drifting further and further away. The poor girl is a mess behind that glamorous smile but not as bad as Madeline. It actually made me laugh when I heard people call her the 'high school sweetheart', if only they knew

Sent by Scarlett at 5:00 A.M.

***

THE TRUTH HURTS. That's the reality of life. It sucked. I guess that why people lied and deceived one another. That's probably why I smiled at the Elites every day as if I wasn't about to ruin their lives. Akari quickly warmed up to me, Kaito's presence got less unsettling and Celeste hated me even more as the days went on.

Nevertheless, they treated me no less than they treated each other; even Madeline began to acknowledge my existence as we'd bond over such basic things like her shoes or my bag. I knew she was trying to get to me, figure out who I was and where was the best place to strike. Was I insecure about myself? Was I involved in drama before I had met them? Who was my last love? Why did they break away with me?

It was all a game, just a simple interaction turned into a game for them. A clear example would be during this one lunchtime where we were all in courtyard, and the weather warm and humid to the point it got disgustingly stuffy in the cafeteria. Celeste claimed that this type of humidity would affect her pores and she'd break out on her face. Sadly, she remained looking flawless as ever.

"I need a drink," she huffed, shifting on the bench and pouting at Bentley. He looked away from his phone, briefly giving her the attention, she wanted before rolling his eyes. That clear meant he wasn't going to get it. Her mood soured immediately after. "Eli, get me a drink."

Elijah, who was quietly sitting on the grass with his full concentration on his laptop, didn't miss a heartbeat as he got up to do as he was instructed. He walked away silently, hands in his pockets, brooding as always. He was a difficult one to read, it irked me. Celeste smiled, glancing at Bentley who was still focused on his phone.

Her smile dropped.

Madeline didn't seem to notice her best friend's bitter mood as she sun-bathed, shades covering her icy blue eyes, blonde hair sprawled across the grass, earphones blocking out the outside sound as she hummed a tune. I sat beside Akari as she coated my nails with metallic red and, although she was focused on what she was doing, she sent me small, amused smirk that said more than words could ever.

Somewhere, during his time away, Elijah must've met Kaito and Zane because the boys walked beside him on his way back; Zane quickly sent me a grin when he saw me. I ducked my head down as I fought back a goofy smile. How pathetic. But Akari didn't waste any time to tease me.

"Aw, you guys are too cute," she cooed, my eyes sending her a glare, but it did nothing, encouraging her to laugh.

"How's my Candy?" Zane greeted, breaking my attention away from the giggling Japanese girl as his arm slugged over my shoulder, taking a seat beside me.

"Hot," I replied. "Did you bring ice cream?"

"Of course!" he answered, waving the plastic bag in his hand.

"A life saver!" Akari squealed as she snatched the bag out his hand, a scowl crossing his face. She paid no attention to the sulking Zane and handed out the ice creams to everyone.

Celeste refused to have any ice creams, claiming it had too much calories and happily drank her iced coffee that Elijah had brought for her, her green cat eyes unwavering from Akari as the Japanese continued to hand out the rest out to everyone else. She was sitting on the table besides Bentley, designer shades on her head, sipping on the cold drink, observing everyone in the courtyard, scowling when she saw some freshmen playing with water balloons.

"You seem to daze off quite a lot, Lowell," Kaito mused, my eyes flickering over to him, the silver haired boy sitting on the grass with that infamous smirk on his face. "What's going on in that pretty little head of yours?"

"Leave her alone, Kai," Zane said with a sigh before I could reply, thankfully. Kaito's unnerving eyes focused on me for a minute longer before he shrugged and looked away. I shifted uncomfortably in my seat, catching Zane's attention. "Ignore him. As I said before, he likes teasing people. You'll get used to it."

"He likes picking on me," I muttered, causing a smile to appear on Zane's face.

"Only because you're easy to tease."

"What's that meant to mean?" I frowned but he didn't give an answer, shrugging with a stupid little smile on his face as he ate his ice cream.

Akari returned back to her seat next to me. "You just proved his point, Candace."

I sulked, amusing both Akari and Zane as they sent a smile to one another. Suddenly, a piercing scream caught everyone's attention, directing their gaze to the culprit. My eyes widened when I saw Celeste absolutely doused from head to toe in water and coffee, stains appearing on her white blouse. Her pristine hair was ruined by the water which must've come from one of the water balloons as the evidence rest on her head. She trembled with anger, snatching the broke rubber from her head and throwing it onto the ground before glancing up, eyes blazing with fury.

"You," she hissed, my eyes glimpsing over to a freshman, who was completely shocked by what occurred but now she had to face the wrath of

Celeste Leon. She stood up in disgust, lips curling into a deep scowl as her hands curled into a tight fist, drenched in water and coffee. "Look at what you have done!"

"I'm so sorry, Celeste!" The young girl cried.

"You should be," Celeste seethed. "Do you know how much one spends on hair and makeup? To look this beautiful?"

"I—"

"Clearly not and it shows," The girl cowered as Celeste loomed over her. "You're pathetic, I hope you know that. It baffles me that someone as incompetent as you not only drenched me in water but also spilled my iced coffee, which I have been dying for all lunch. You have not only ruined my lunch and my look but congratulation, you've ruined my mood as well."

The girl clasped her hands together, tears streaming down her face, yet no one stood up for her. Zane silently sat beside me; Akari looked at the ground with her eyes closed as if it would make it all disappear. Madeline and Kaito watched in amusement, Elijah completely unbothered whilst Bentley remained interested with his phone. And they let her cry as she was humiliated.

My heart clenched in both anger and sadness; my fists curled so tightly I was pretty sure they became white. As if he knew my thoughts, Zane gripped onto my wrist tightly, the arm around my shoulder preventing me from moving. I glanced at him with shock, but he didn't pay any attention.

Celeste looked as if she wanted to scratch the girl's face and I wouldn't be surprised if she did as she snapped, "So what are you going to do?"

The girl stuttered as she looked everywhere frantically but came with no answer, the words lost a she quivered in panic.

"Useless. Completely useless," she scoffed. "Ugly, pathetic and now useless. You just ticked all the boxes to be with the lowest of the low. Have fun. You belong with them, freak."

The girl sobbed as she shook her head profusely, "Please, Celeste. Please don't do this."

"Stop whining, it actually pathetic," Celeste scowled, the freshman shaking under her intimidating gaze.

Bentley, who finally looked up from his phone, observed the situation and walked towards her, before murmuring lowly to Celeste. Whatever he said made her even madder, causing her to clench her jaw as the brunette stared in fear, shaking tremendously. Her eyes flashed dangerously as they morphed into slits that could put someone six feet under. Bentley shifted his attention on the freshman, tucking his phone into his pocket.

"I don't appreciate what you have done to my girlfriend," he began, his tone cold and deadly. "I'd be grateful if you could make it up to her, rather than stand there and make a fool of yourself."

The freshman gulped, Celeste stared emotionlessly at the young girl, her arms crossed over her coffee stained blouse, a top that cost the same amount as a Louis Vuitton bag.

"H–how can I–I make it up to–to you, Celeste?" The girl stuttered.

"Give her your blouse," Bentley stated, his face gave away no expressions. The freshman looked baffled, her mouth opening and closing as if she was loss for words. Rolling his eyes, the irritation clear when his jaw flexed, he repeated his words. "Give her your blouse."

"N–now?" she whispered, fearfully. Fearing her reputation, fearing humiliation, fearing Celeste and Bentley. "Maybe we can go to the bathroom and—"

"No," A sharp and abrupt answer, cutting off the stream of words that would leave the freshman's rosy lips. Bentley's word was an order, a command. "Now."

At first, the girl was hesitant, fiddling with her buttons, until she glanced up to see Bentley's murky brown eyes thinned into shards and Celeste lips pursed together as she narrowed her eyes with expectations. With a shaky sigh, her eyes watering up, she began to unbutton her white blouse, slipping off her tanned shoulders with wobbly hands until she stood in the courtyard in just her bra and skirt. Bentley looked satisfied, the corner of his lips coiling into a mocking grin when she held the blouse out.

"Now, that wasn't hard," he said, snatching the blouse out of the freshman's hand, turning to Celeste. "My love?"

Celeste gradually moved her focus away from the young girl and onto the blouse, grasping it into her hands. For a second, she looked guilty, disheartened, but it quickly morphed into amusement as she scrutinised the petite girl under her beady green cat eyes.

"Much appreciated. Although, next you should rethink your bra choices. Pink hearts don't really suit you," she taunted. The freshman's cheek burned red, flushed in embarrassment as scatter of laughter spread across the courtyard. "I believe we are done here."

Although, Celeste was done tormenting, from the way Bentley' eyes twinkled, I knew he was far from done. Brown discs turned to the direction of the slim blonde Elite, who was witnessing the event quietly. As if she knew what he was about to ask, or order, she stumbled onto her feet.

"How about we show our friend here a taste of her own medicine?" he suggested, hauntingly. "Could you do us the honours?"

Coral lips frowned as Celeste stared at her boyfriend in bewilderment. But Madeline knew what he was asking, I knew what he was asking. My heart sank. I wasn't sure if Madeline wanted to do it, I don't think she was but the dark look across Bentley's face would make anyone think twice before arguing. Blue eyes glanced at another freshman, who trembled with dread as she gestured to hand her a water balloon.

"Zane," I whispered with wide eyes, but he hushed me softly, shaking his head as he watched with sorrow in his eyes. "We can't just do nothing."

"That's the thing, Candace," he answered quietly. "Nothing is all we can do."

The brunette frowned, momentarily, not scared, but baffled to what Bentley said that she didn't realised what was happening until it happened. The water balloon hit her with such force that it made her stumble back and trip over her own foot, causing her to fall and shocking us all when her hair — no, her wig came off. My hand covered my mouth in shock as a scatter of gasps echoed throughout the courtyard, whilst the brunette staggered back onto her feet, her face burning red as she clutched onto the brown wig tightly against her chest, tears staining her cheeks. Madeline laughed, crossing her arms over her chest as she rose a brow in delight. Bentley looked satisfied, relishing in the humiliation of the young girl, who was currently sobbing as she clutched onto her wig, hundreds of piranhas watching her.

"Well, well," he teased. "What do we have here? Looks revolting, wouldn't you agree, Celeste?"

Something flashed so quickly in Celeste's eyes that if you weren't pay attention you wouldn't have seen it, but, like always, I saw everything, and I knew that she was surprised as well. It was so brief. A miniscule of a second. Before it dispersed and was replaced with amusement, taunting the freshman, ridiculing her as she crushed the girl's self-confidence in front of everyone in the courtyard.

"Perhaps, ugly isn't the right word to use," she paused before peering down at the girl then smirking. "Revolting does seem to fit better."

Her words stung and it was all she had left to say. The girl shook before running away, crying in humiliation. After a long, cold minute, Celeste didn't look the least bit satisfied as she spun, eyes glaring at Bentley.

"Happy?"she asked, taking me by surprise. He smirked before shrugging, uninterestedly, but that only infuriated her even more. "You ba—"

His eyes sharpened to a scary glare, daggers that could put someone six feet under, it even caused Celeste to tense. "Stop right there. You didn't have to do, or say, anything you didn't want to. And, from the looks of it, you enjoyed it more than you'd admit."

"Did you actually just say that with a straight face?" she laughed bitterly, Zane tensing besides me and his hold on my wrist tightened.

Bentley's eyes flashed dangerously when he stood up straighter, towering over her when his fists curled up and jaw clenched. I noticed her submit slightly, almost cowering when he did this; it was such a shock that I couldn't stop the gasp from escaping my lips. I knew he had held power over her but seeing it happen right in front of me made me hold my breath, the tension suffocating the group. She held his gaze, even if she was trembling unnoticeably, but after a moment of battling dominance, he won and she looked away, clenching and unclenching her jaw.

"We are done here," he said, darkly, his tone dropping a few notches that when he spoke, it caused me to shudder. His brown, murky eyes scrutinized everyone in the courtyard, forcing them to look away in fear of facing his wrath before they settled onto his girlfriend. "Celeste?"

She didn't even hesitate, slipping her hand into his outstretched one before they walked away: The King and the Queen. Madeline's smile was long gone, observing their retreating back before glancing at the freshmen, and then at me. She was unreadable, impassive to what just occurred; maybe because it happened so frequently that they had gotten used to it. She held my gaze, her azure eyes darkening before a sigh left her lips, running her fingers through her blonde locks.

"Let's leave," she said. "It's getting too crowded in here."

The remaining Elites, excluding Zane, murmured in agreement, gathering their things before following after her when she walked off. Zane's shoulders slugged once they all disappeared into the building, and I glanced at him, speechless to what just occurred but, even then, he sorrowfully shook his head, refusing to give the answer I needed, and walked away with his hands in his pockets.

-

What do you think of our Harrington Elites?

- fariha.

09 | scandalous

Chapter IX: Scandalous

I knew there was something suspicious about that girl. No girl can have hair that blonde and luscious without hiding secrets underneath it. Madeline confuses me, I don't understand why she is called the 'high school sweetheart'. What about her is sweet? To me, she's just a blonder and skinnier version of Celeste.

How can someone gain a nickname so innocent and be anything but?

Sent by Candace at 9:30 A.M.

***

IT WAS A COUPLE weeks after the entire fiasco happened. In fact, it was like it had never happened. The girl who was brutally humiliated and degraded by Celeste was pulled out of Harrington; no one knew where she went. Sometimes, you'd hear whispers of gossip and the hushed conversations between cliques as you walked down the corridors, but they were all quickly silenced, especially if you were unlucky and caught by one of the Elites.

I had no doubt that Bentley was the main reason behind it all; he'd sit smugly besides Celeste whenever Madeline brought news that another student had dropped out of Harrington, and sometimes — if he was in a bad mood — they were humiliated first.

The other week, Akari told me how a red-haired junior was retelling the events to her boyfriend, who'd been off sick for a couple of days, whilst her so–called friends were around. They wasted no time on snitching on her. Why they did it could be due to a numerous of reasons: to get into Celeste's good books, to join the Wannabes, to be invited to exclusive parties, to gain all the advantages the green–eyed goddess can offer them. Although, why they did it didn't matter. The red-headed 's boyfriend broke up with her that very same day publicly and, in less than 5 minutes, had his arm around another girl. Celeste leapt at the opportunity to break down the girl's self–esteem and Bentley... He shamelessly handed a wad of cash to her ex-boyfriend right in front of her.

You couldn't trust anyone here; everyone had their own agendas.

And I fit perfectly in.

*

The weather in New York dramatically changed. The occasional sunshine and warm weather were quickly replaced with grey skies and frost biting against the leaves and trees. I sat in the library, mindlessly playing with my pen as I formulated my next plan. Since the discovery of Katio's illegal expenditures, I'd been at stalemate as I hadn't had the chance to return to the club — Akari refused to come along especially after her brother had gotten mad at her for going in the first place. I groaned in annoyance and rested my head on the table, grumbling profanities to myself.

"Why did you do this to me, Scar?" I grumbled. "Because of you, I had to become friends with Elites, do you know how painful that is?"

"No, but I'd like to find out."

My head shot up at the unknown voice, wide eyes staring at the boy with shaggy ebony hair, who leaned against a bookshelf with his arms crossed over his chest whilst he smirked at me. He wore a long overcoat that matched with the black jeans and white shirt underneath. I had never seen or meet him before, but he looked strangely familiar. Albeit, that didn't stop my heart from plummeting and all I could think was that this was the end, and I had failed Scarlett.

"Excuse me?"

"You know at first I didn't believe it," he said instead, slipping into the seat opposite me. "But now, I definitely see it."

Narrowing my eyes suspiciously, I asked, "See what?"

"How similar you are to Scarlett."

"Excuse me?" I repeated, unable to stop the stunned look across my face.

His smirk widened as he bent forward, clasping his hands together on the table. "You're Scarlett's best friend."

"Stop saying that name," I hissed quietly.

"What? Scarlett?" he taunted and frowned playfully as he cocked his head to the side, feigning innocence. "You don't like me saying Scarlett Lock—"

I leaned forward, glaring daggers at the unknown boy, seething, "I swear to God, you repeat that name one more time and I won't hesitate in ensuring your dismissal from this school."

He chuckled, entertained by my threat. "I know you have the power too, but I also know you won't do that."

I kept my eyes on him steadily, unsure of what was his game and his true intentions. My guard was up like a skyscraper and, although I promised I'd never abuse my authority and power, I knew that if he was to ruin my plan, there'd be some sacrifices I was open to make.

"And why is that?"

His brown eyes twinkled knowingly, lips curving into a Cheshire grin. "Because you need me."

It was silent for a moment as I studied him, leaning back with my arms crossed over my chest. It could all be a joke, a ploy, something that Celeste had set up to catch me in the act. Or maybe Bentley — I wouldn't put it past him. Yet, in all honesty, a part of me knew that I wasn't caught so with a defeated sigh and a roll of my eyes, I raised a brow expectantly, which only caused him to broaden his smile.

"I knew Scarlett before she became one of the Elites, I was quite close with her back when she was only in 'the third clique', I believed she had called them," he began. "She mentioned you quite a few times, she kept going on about her friend in England who was so sweet and kind or how you would hate Harrington because of the people within it."

"You're not only testing my patience, you're also in the third clique. A group known to never be involved with the Elites," I snapped. "You better get to the point before I reconsider my decision of listening to you."

With slightly narrowed eyes, he chortled. "She did say you had a hot–temper."

"Did she also tell you how mad I'm getting right now?"

"You know, you should be more friendly to people who are offering to help you take the Elites down. Not many people would do that," he retorted, a scoff escaping my lips.

"I don't need your help."

"Yes, you do because I'm the only one that knew of Scarlett's little plan before everyone else did. I helped her formulate the plan and when it came crashing down, when she went haywire, I left her," His words held weight to it, it was visible in the way he slugged his shoulders. He inhaled sharply, glancing away from me. "I can't stop seeing her, Candace. I regret giving up on her too early. That's why I want to help."

I hesitated shortly before asking, "How did you help her?"

"She quickly caught the interest of the Elites, far quicker than the usual student would. When she got the eighth seat to the table, for some time, it was peaceful, and she told me how enjoyable it was whenever we'd meet. But, even to this day, I still don't understand why she switched. She came to me one night, tears streaking down her face, and told me how much she hated the Elites and wanted to destroy them," His eyes glazed over as if he was recalling the memory, causing him to a pull a face.

"She never told you why?"

He shook his head. "Not once. Every time I'd ask, she'd avoid the conversation."

I sighed, rubbing my forehead as I felt a headache beginning to form. "If we are to work together, you need to tell me everything you know. Do you understand?"

He pondered for a moment before breaking into a huge grin as he stood up, tucking his hands into his coat pockets. "I look forward to working with you, Candace."

As he walked away, I quickly realised that I didn't even know his name.

"Wait!" I yelled, catching his attention as he came to a halt, slowly glancing over his shoulder. "You didn't even tell me your name."

"Harris," he replied. "Harris Clermont."

*

Celeste had a boyfriend. That was a fact. Madeline had a boyfriend. Now, that was a rumour. And usually rumours were right. On the way to AP History, I overheard a small group of sophomores that were huddled around each other near their lockers. It perked up my curiosity almost instantaneously the second I heard her name.

"Did you hear that Madeline is seeing someone?" someone said.

"I heard she met him over summer," someone else muttered.

"Apparently he's older than her."

Someone snorted in amusement. "Clearly she has a type."

Madeline is known to keep her relationships on the downlow; sometimes, she'd be in a six–month relationship and no one would know, even if they broke up as well. She was secretive when it came to her own personal affairs but when it involved other people, she was usually the source of the news. So, hearing a rumour like this needed to be confirmed and I had full intentions of doing so. During History, something one of the girls said bothered me, it didn't make sense and I knew after investigating into it I'd get my answers, and who better to go to than Akari?

My friendship with Akari had developed a lot since I first met her especially as her relationship with Celeste had started to deteriorate. It was almost too easy to use that to my advantage; her insecurities were almost too easy to play with. I did everything I could to manipulate her into believing

Celeste didn't respect her, that she was no one of importance to the Elites, that she could be dismissed easily by them. The fun part of it all was that she believed me. However, what irked me was her loyalty to Celeste was unaffected despite the seeds of betrayal I planted in her thoughts. It made me wonder if she would break any time soon.

"Can you stop doing that?" Madeline muttered in exasperation, breaking my train of thought.

I glanced over to her with a frown before my eyes followed her gaze onto my leg that shook in agitation. Unfortunately, fate (fate being our History Teacher, Mr Harding) decided to have me sitting beside Madeline during the lesson for the rest of the year, especially as I was one of the top students in his class and she, on the other hand... well, she wasn't doing too good.

Sheepishly, I smiled. "Sorry."

She muttered something incomprehensively as she turned away from me. My eyes remained steadily focusing on her as I took in her features; her blue eyes that looked like ice, her blonde hair almost the same colour as gold, her high cheekbones that accentuated her jawline, in other words she looked like the perfect Barbie doll. Ephemerally, it made me contemplate whether she was this villain that Scarlett painted her out to be.

"God, Madeline can be such a cow sometimes," Scarlett grumbled through the phone speakers whilst I was doing my makeup. Outside, the sky began to darken as the sun was hidden behind the showers and the grey clouds, however for Scar, the sun was still out, greeting New York with warm weather and clear skies.

"What did she do now?" I asked, tinting my lips in pink.

Scarlett sighed. "She made me return this beautiful dress I bought because she had the same one. Did I mention it was beau–ti–ful?"

"Why would she do that?"

"Like I said a cow. She's just entitled, being Celeste's best friend gives her more rights than anyone else in the Elites," she huffed. "Sometimes I just want to rip off her blonde extensions off."

That caused me to smile. "She has extensions?"

Scarlett giggled, my heart warming at the sound of her laugh, it always brightened my day. "Yeah! And she goes around telling people that it's real when its anything but."

"What is it?" Madeline snapped, flickering her eyes over to me. "Why are you staring at me?"

My thoughts quickly shattered when I finally acknowledged her, shaking my head as I forced a smile. "Sorry, lost in my thoughts."

Suspiciously, she held my gaze as if she didn't believe me, although I didn't blame her; her lack of friendship towards me stemmed mainly due to her best friend's hatred towards my presence in the group. Eventually, she curled her lips in dislike before rolling her eyes distastefully, muttering under her breath, "Freak."

When her attention was someplace else, my eyes sharpened into blades that promised to put her and her reputation six feet under before shifting my focus back onto our teacher, clenching tightly to the pen in my hand.

Maybe Scarlett was right. Perhaps she was a cow.

*

On the way to the cafeteria, I couldn't stop replaying what I had overheard which, consequently, led me into knocking into Harris, my bag sliding off my shoulder, causing the contents within it to spill across the marble flooring. Lurching back, because I lost a sense of balance, his hand quickly shot out, winding around my wrist and hauling me into his arm; the minimal distance between us caused my breath to hitch.

"Are you okay?" he muttered lowly, nonchalantly, despite the little distance between us. Flustered, I nodded before jerking away from him when I realised we were being watched.

Rubbing my arm, I mumbled, "Yeah, I'm okay."

He studied me warily before bending down, collecting my belongings together whilst people around us whispered and murmured. Harris didn't seem like he cared about the attention as he continued to grab my things before standing back up, handing my bag to me with a sheepish look on his face.

"Sorry," he said as I took the bag from him.

"As I said, I'm okay."

"Let me walk you to the cafeteria," Harris suggested.

"You know I can't do that," I answered before walking away from him, but that didn't stop him from quickly catching up with me, his hand gripping onto my arm, tugging me to face him. The corner of his lips quirked up as he rose a brow, his indigo eyes glittering when he saw the irritation on my face. "Let me go. Someone is going to see us, Harris, and I'd rather prefer our interactions to be kept private."

He rolled his eyes. "I have something to give you."

I frowned. "What is it?"

Opening his mouth to speak, he was cut off by someone else, my eyes glancing over to the owner of the voice.

"What are you doing?"

Zane stood behind us, at the entrance of the cafeteria, with his murky grey eyes narrowed as they observed the current situation, a small frown creeping onto his lips. My heart plunged in dread, but I did my best to keep my composure as I shook off Harris's hold on my arm, stepping away from him so there was a reasonable distance between us. I couldn't get caught, not when I got this far, I refuse to be caught.

"Nothing," I countered, moving closer to Zane, my hands snaking around his upper arm; I smiled at him innocently before sending a sharp look towards Harris, who challengingly held Zane's gaze. "Harris is in one of my lessons and just wanted to give me the folder I left in class."

Zane's steel grey eyes didn't waver from Harris when he said, "I didn't know you were still around, Clermont. Didn't they kick you out?"

Harris crossed his arms over his chest, raising a brow. "My father convinced them otherwise. Sound familiar, Stryker?"

Whatever Harris was trying to imply clear set Zane off as his entire body tensed up, his jaw clenching as he tightened his fists until they turned white, his eyes glaring daggers as if they were knives.

"Stay away from us, Clermont, if you know what's good for you," Zane warned. "Unless you prefer to be in the lower cliques or maybe in a slightly more.... deceased situation."

I watched the interaction between the boys with confusion but didn't let go of Zane's arm in fear that he'd hurt Harris. The corridor was silent, my mind suddenly acknowledging the other students around us, who watched meticulously at what was occurring, occasionally whispering to each other but that only heightened my anxiety until it felt like I couldn't breathe. My heart clenched as I swallowed nervously. It felt like hours had passed by before Harris chuckled as he rose his hands in surrender, backing away with a glimmer of amusement in his eyes.

"Heard the message loud and clear," His focus shifted over to me before he sent a cheeky wink. "See you around, Candace."

His hands tucked into his coat pocket, he sauntered down the corridor which finally allowed me to exhale the breath of air was I was holding in. Zane didn't move even after Harris disappear around the corner; his fists remained clenched tightly, his body tensed as he continued to remain on guard.

"Zane?" I whispered, tugging his arm softly. His eyes glazed over as they flickered to me but, eventually, he relaxed, his shoulder slugging as if the stress on them was finally removed. "Are you okay?"

"Yeah, I am," he exhaled before taking my hands into his. "Promise me you'll stay away from him, Candace."

Furrowing my brows, I frowned. "What? Why?"

"Just promise me, Candace."

"Okay, okay. I promise."

Zane's facial expression finally softened and soon I was gifted with a smile, his facial muscles loosening and his grey eyes sparkling once again.

"Come on, the rest of our friends are waiting for us."

*

Once the final bell rang, signalling that this long and eventful day was finally over, I quickly darted out of my Math classroom and travelled through the school building, determined to find my History teacher to get his intake on the images of the cultural relics that Kaito was illegally selling, and find out whether they were authentic or not. Muttering out apologises whenever I accidently bumped into people, I didn't want to waste any time in case I lost him, so I didn't focus much on who was around me. Finally, I got to the section of Harrington where all the humanities classrooms were, stopping temporarily to catch my breath.

Swiftly, I took my phone out my bag, scrolling onto my gallery as I made my way to the classroom where I expected to find him but, just as I reached the door handle, I came to a halt, glancing up to the small window in the door, my eyes widening when I witnessed the situation occurring in front of me. I almost dropped my phone when I covered my mouth to prevent the gasp escaping my lips. After the initial shock was over, my lips curved into a sadistic smile as I carefully took a snapshot of what was happening, amused by how well everything was panning out to be.

Cautiously, I stepped backwards away from the door before strolling away, glancing down at the compromising image on my phone.

An image of Madeline lip-locked with our history teacher.

-

It's not a scandalous book without a teacher–student relationship.

xoxo,

- fariha.

10 | room 125

Chapter X: Room 125

The nickname began in freshman year, when Zane was teasing her and calling her a people-pleaser. Although, he wasn't wrong; Madeline loved to do whatever she needed to do to ensure that she had the admiration and love from others. Since then, she's had become the face of Harrington; star pupil, the best grades and let's not forget, drop-dead gorgeous. Celeste might be the Queen of Harrington, but Madeline is the main reason there's so many applicants to enter the school; she was the first student parents would be introduced to.

But, you know as well as I do, that this is all just a deception. It's an illusion that plays perfectly well for Harrington Preparatory and the main reason why Celeste is the downfall for so many students. Madeline is conniving. If she wants something, she will do everything in power to get it.

Sent by Scarlett at 6:00 P.M.

***

BEST GRADES? Yet, another lie.

Over the past two weeks, after discovering Madeline's little secret, I did my best in ensuring I had enough footage and evidence regarding our history teacher and Madeline's affair. I'd keep an eye on her locations prior to school and where she disappeared off to after school. On most occasions she'd return home, but I noticed that twice a week, she'd visit The Carlyle, one of the most luxe hotels in New York due to being situated on the Upper East and its famous view of the city skyline.

At first, I didn't think anything of it until one night I noticed Mr Harding, looking slightly out of place, as he checked himself in at the reception. I had sat in the foyer; shades covering my eyes, a thin, satin scarf covering my hair, a white dress clinging onto my body and my favourite pair of Christian Louboutin's to complete the look. Feigning interest, I flicked through pages of magazine, but my focus was entirely on Mr Harding.

From what I had gathered, Madeline would arrive exactly at seven in the evening which would give an hour gap between her check in and our history teacher's. He wasn't as precise as her. Sometimes he'd check in before eight, sometimes he'd check after eight. Nevertheless, one factor which remained consistent was that he'd ask for keys to the same room every time.

"Room 125," I smirked.

The room was recently attended to by the maids, the scent of fresh linen perfumed the room, a warm and cosy ambience greeting you the second you stepped in. After carefully inspecting the area, I glanced at the clock, noticing that Madeline's arrival would be soon and decided to make my presence unknown before she caught me.

Instead of putting my plan motion, I knew that it wasn't the right time just yet, hence how I ended up spending my Thursday evening with Akari.

I was sitting in bed, glasses propped on top of my head, homework that was set today was discarded to the side as I scrolled through my Instagram, when Akari's name popped up on my screen, a familiar ringtone trilling from the device in my hand. I rolled my eyes before I answered.

"Hey."

"Are you busy?" she demanded, ignoring my greeting. I blinked at her straightforwardness, hesitating to give an answer.

"Erm— yeah?" I cringed at how my reply sounded more like a question than an answer.

"So, you can't come over?"

"No."

I could almost visualise her rolling her eyes before she replied, "Does that mean I have to come to you?"

"Can I ask why?"

"I'll explain when I come over," she insisted before hanging up, giving me no chance to dispute back as I glanced at my phone blankly.

As I was making my room presentable to an Elite's standard, a sudden wave of unease hit like a tsunami and I stopped what I was doing, furrowing my brows in discomfort. It would the first time an Elite entered my home, a place I deemed sacred, somewhere I can retreat in times of stress and uncertainty and, here I was allowing someone who has the power to disrupt that peace into my safe place.

It's not like I could anything about it now because when I finally snapped out of my daze, the doorbell rang. A huge part of me hoped that it was my mother, but I knew that it wouldn't been as she was working late. The other part of me was dumbfound to how quickly Akari had arrived, especially how I didn't inform her about my address — though I wouldn't be surprised if it was due to Kaito's doing.

When I opened the door, she greeted me with a bright grin, waving a bag of McDonald's in front of me. As always, she looked flawless as ever. Her sepia hair was neatly tied back, and she wore a pastel pink dress that accentuated her figure faultlessly, lips coated in red, similar to the tint on her cheek.

"Hey, Candace."

"Akari," I greeted, further opening the door to allow her to enter. There was this brief moment of hesitation before she stepped inside, glancing around with judgemental eyes. I noticed them narrow before relaxing, a look of surprise flickering through them before dispersing. "I never told you where I lived. How did you find me so quickly?"

She glanced over her shoulders. "Kaito has a record of every students' address in Harrington."

Told you.

"I bought dinner. Usually, I'm not too fond of eating food like this, especially when I'm trying to maintain my body and health, but Celeste pissed me off considerably today, so I needed food comfort," she gestured to the bag before pouting. "I hope you haven't eaten yet."

"I'm always hungry for McDonalds," I answered, earning a little squeal of happiness from her. "Shall we head upstairs?"

Her eyes didn't waver as they fixated on everything, even the smallest of details, oblivious that I kept looking back at her when she didn't answer my questions. Eventually, we got to my bedroom, her eyes enlarged in surprise before she grinned at me with approval.

"Am I the first to come in here? You look a bit on edge," Akari mused as she kicked her heels off, taking a seat on my bed.

"How did you guess?" I smiled guiltily.

Her eyes widened in astonishment, "Are you serious? Not even Zane? I would've thought at least Zane would've come here."

I pulled a face. "Akari, why are you here?"

Her lips coiled into a smirk when she noticed me deflecting the attention onto her but didn't continue to make any further comments. Shrugging, she began to eat the chips in the bag after handing out the food to me when I finally settled onto the bed besides her.

"The usual; Celeste," she huffed. "It's so aggravating having to listen to her orders when she doesn't even consider me to be one of her friends. Did I tell you that we used to be pretty close? Madeline, Celeste and I were so tight, I just don't understand what happened. She disappeared during the end of Sophomore year. No one heard from her all summer, but when she came back at the start of Junior year, it was like her and I were never friends. It just didn't make sense."

"Celeste isn't the type of person to cut people off without a valid reason," I replied.

"No. No, she isn't."

"Something must've happened for her to distance herself away from you."

Akari sighed and for the first time, I realised how tired she looked. Underneath her eyes was dark bags, the usual spark of light within her eyes slightly diminished, there was a noticeable slouch as if keeping a straight posture was arduous and her fingers slowly drummed against her thighs.

I never wanted to feel remorse towards the Elites, but Akari reminded me how Scarlett once looked like. It was exhausting to meet up with the demands and expectations of the Elites, especially when you had not only Celeste watching you, but everyone in Harrington. Being powerful and popular wasn't prodigious as it seemed.

"It doesn't matter anymore," she muttered sorrowfully. There was this melancholy silence between us before she smiled softly at me. "At least I have you now."

If it was even possible, I was pretty sure my heart cracked in agony whilst I smiled at her. I couldn't bring myself to lie and instead diverted the conversation to something else.

"I have something to tell you, but you need to promise you won't tell anyone," she nodded eagerly, scooting closer to me. "I saw Madeline with our history teacher. Is that who she's in a relationship with?"

Akari's face whitened as shock settled over her, her eyes dilated before she glanced away, "You shouldn't have seen that."

"So, I'm right?" Tentatively, she grimaced with a small nod. "I can't believe that. She could get in so much trouble."

"Don't be too surprised. She does this all the time, most the time it's when she needs to bump her grades up. Madeline isn't exactly the smartest, you know."

"She sleeps with her teachers to raise her grades? Is that how she's been passing her tests?"

"Yeah. Although, there was this one summer where she went completely off the grid and apparently was at some summer school, at least that's what Mrs Vos told everyone. Coincidentally enough, one of our best math teachers had resigned around the same time. Between you and me, she definitely spent summer abroad with him. I don't think she was with him for the grades, I'm pretty sure they were in a serious relationship."

"How can you say that for sure?"

"It was just before Celeste disappeared," Akari responded. "Celeste mentioned it briefly to me but never went into detail however, it wasn't difficult to piece everything together. Especially, when—"

She stopped midway as if she had realised something before shaking her head after a brief moment passed by, gifting me a radiant smile. Noticing the small frown that made itself known on my face, she laughed, nudging me playfully.

"In time, Candace."

"What does that mean?" I demanded.

"It means that it's time to watch a film," Hopping off the bed, she moved towards my shelf of films, distracting herself and evading my questions like usual.

*

My conversation with Akari provided me deeper insight and understanding towards Madeline's action; it made perfectly sense. With high expectations from Mrs Vos and now her new stepfather, Mr Harrington, Madeline had to secure all possible chances of being accepted into the best Universities and guarantee that her prestigious reputation remained intact. It made this all more entertaining.

To my knowledge, Madeline and Mr Harding would meet again on Tuesday so, that very evening, dressed in looks that screamed revenge, I went to the reception where I asked for the keys to room 125. Of course, the receptionist knew I wasn't Madeline but, after some convincing, she handed me the keys.

Smiling politely, I took them out of her hands before sauntering towards the lift, leading me to the floor where room 125 was situated. I glanced at my watch, noticing that it was only six and decided to send a quick text to Harris as his help would be crucial in guaranteeing this plan ran through smoothly.

In less than a minute, he answered back confirming that Madeline wouldn't arrive anytime soon which lifted a huge weight off my shoulders; I didn't want to know how he was able to keep her away nor did I care, he completed his job and that was all that mattered. Tucking my phone back into my purse, I slowly opened the door, noticing that it had remained untouched, prepared and ready for its regular guests. I placed my bag on top of the vanity, pouring myself a glass of wine before settling onto the couch against the window.

The sun was barely up, hidden behind the vast skyscrapers in the city, however, the sky was beautiful mix of red and orange, an illusion that the sky was set alight. I might have been high up in the building, but I could still hear the busy New York streets, vehicles driving parallel to each other as everyone rushed to head home after a busy day.

It wasn't an unusual sight; back in England, the streets in Central London were hectic and buzzing with life. It was something I loved dearly about cities. The impression it left was long-lasting. Equally like Scarlett. The horizon reminded me of her fiery, red hair and the busy streets remained me of her charismatic personality, she was larger than life itself.

I wasn't too sure how time quickly passed by, I guess I was too invested with the scenery that only when I heard the door rattle, it broke me out of my spell. I noted that it was five past eight. The door opened, shedding light to the dark room, and Mr Harding entered. It was no lie that he was attractive.

He was one of the young teachers in Harrington, who was exceptionally smart and considerate.

His brunet hair was groomed neatly and carefully that it had a rippling quality. The aquiline nose he sported complemented his prominent cheekbones. Dressed in a black suit, his aura spoke power and strength yet, it baffled me that someone like him ended up falling into Madeline Vos's perfectly manicured hands. I almost felt guilty about what I was going to do.

Almost.

"Babe, why is it so dark—" Mr Harding cut himself short once he turned the lights on, my presence startling him. He blinked in confusion. "Candace?"

"Good evening, Sir," I smiled innocently, sitting comfortably with the small glass of wine in my hand, one leg crossed over the other.

Cautiously, his eyes flickered down the corridor before closing the door behind him. I fought back the urge to laugh at his dumfound expression when he glanced around the room — most likely searching for Madeline but, with the help of Harris, she wouldn't make it this evening.

"What is this?" he asked.

"How about you tell me?" I gestured to the empty spare glass on the table. "Wine?"

He shook his head with a frown. "I don't think that's appropriate."

I rolled my eyes and continued to pour the red liquid into the wine glass, unfaltering even as I felt his restless eyes examine me. Once I was done, I held it out to him, my smile unwavering. "You're going to want this."

At first, Mr Harding was hesitant, trying to hide the uneasy expression that was slowly, but surely, masking his face. He eventually took the glass with shaky hands.

"Once again, Miss Lowell, may I ask what's going on?"

"Miss Lowell? Are we going with formalities now?" With a brow raised, I shook my head in disapproval. "Is that what you call Madeline?"

His face paled, eyes widening as he gaped at me to my amusement.

"I'm quite disappointed, Mr Harding. Or can I call you Richard instead? I assume that's what Maddie calls you," He didn't answer, slowly settling onto the edge of the bed, his eyes did not move its attention away from me. "A relationship with a Madeline Vos. Bear in mind, not only has she not turned eighteen but she's also your student, in fact your failing student. Which leads me to the question on whether you're improving her grades as long as she remained in a very, illegal relationship with you."

I sighed. "Statutory rape, I believe it's called. Let's not forget sexual coercion. Something like that can get you on the sex offenders list very quickly, and that wouldn't be a pretty look for you once Harrington Preparatory kicks you out."

He didn't speak for the longest time, my threat settling over him. For a brief second, I felt nauseous and my anxiety causing my body to betray me. Nevertheless, I did my best to keep my composure, refusing to give in and ensure that I stuck through with my plan. Although I was lacking in confidence with power, I was the best in acting like I had so much of it and, from the way Mr Harding studied me cautiously, I knew he believed it too.

His eyes narrowed. "Why do I get the feeling that you don't intend on telling anyone about it?"

I smirked.

"Because I don't," I responded. "I can't lose my favourite teacher now, can I?"

"What do you want?" he sighed in defeat.

"It's simple actually. If you do it, I'll keep my lips sealed and no one will ever find out your dirty little secret," He looked at me expectantly, my smirk widening. "You need to ensure that Madeline fails History."

"And why would I do that?"

"Because, you and me both know that this little fling will be the downfall to your reputation. Are you really willing to ruin your life worth of hard work for a girl who gets everything handed to her on a silver platter?" He didn't answer and he didn't need to, I had him exactly where I wanted him and, without a doubt, I knew he was going to do what was expected of him. I stood up, grabbing my bag on the vanity before glancing down at him.

"I look forward to seeing these results, Mr Harding."

With that said, I left the room.

*

It's difficult to say how committed I was in guaranteeing that the Elites had a damaging downfall that not even their PRs and money would be able to save them. Most days I'd spend to planning my next move whether it was on Madeline or the next person on my list. As time went on, my list progressively got smaller. It was an addiction. The thought of seeing the Elites merciless was gratifying. It wasn't until one Monday, a few days before the winter formal, that my desire to destroy the Elites was fuelled even more.

I was in the library, returning a couple of books I'd taken out for use, when I noticed Harris in the far back of the library, and whoever he was arguing with was hidden behind the large bookshelves sturdily standing along with the other bookshelves, facing parallel to each other. My lips curled down as I inched closer and quietly. I couldn't risk getting caught so I pressed myself against the bookshelf, hidden behind the looming shadow of the wooden object.

"Leave her alone," Harris hissed venomously, his fists clenched tightly until they looked white.

"Why would I do that?" My frown deepened when I recognised the owner of the voice. "She's such a pretty, little toy to play with."

"I swear to God, Elijah. I'm going to knock that smug grin off your face. Back off her."

Elijah laughed darkly. "Your threats mean nothing, Clermont. In fact, I believe it's you who needs to back off or do you need a remind? Was Zane's warning not enough for you?"

"Not if it involves my little sister," Harris growled, the fury evidently clear in his tone.

"Aw, Harris. What happened to us? We used to be brothers and now you can barely stand me."

"That was before my sister and let's not forget that red-head that once sat in your table last year," Harris chuckled. "Or have you forgotten about her? Especially how you all were so quick to replace her."

Elijah was quick to reply, snapping with hatred dripping off his tone, "I suggest you stop speaking, Clermont, or I promise you'll find your sister in a much worse situation."

The threat was clear, holding raw depravity and malicious intent. Harris didn't reply.

"I believe we are done here," Elijah spoke first. "Now, please excuse me, I have a date. Give your sister my love."

I heard Elijah's muffled footsteps disappear into the distance until all that was left was an ominous, sombre silence. I held my breath, trying to take in this sudden wave of new information. I couldn't see Harris be friends with someone like Elijah, it seemed too surreal. But, I guess I kept underestimating everyone at Harrington and this just proved it.

"You can come out now."

I jumped at the sound of Harris's voice, a voice that spoke directly at me. My eyes widened and I peeked in his direction, noticing how his back was still to me and contemplated whether I should walk away or find out what happened. However, I eventually moved out the shadow, the fluorescent lights acted like a spotlight and the sudden urge to shiver rushed over me as if the temperature had dropped dramatically, goose bumps prickling my arms.

"How much of that did you hear?" he asked.

I hesitated before answering, "Quite a bit."

He peered over his shoulders, dark brown eyes scrutinizing me. "I guess you have questions."

"A few."

There was a ghost of a smile before he looked away. "We were close friends, more like brothers. This was before Scarlett, before... He was someone I could trust despite the fact that he was part of the Elites. People weren't when they said he was a saint, they only Elite with humanity. Eli was an honest man."

"What happened?"

"He saw more to life than honesty. He found enjoyment in other people's undoing, he saw how easily he could hurt someone, how easily he could abuse his power and he hurt people. He hurt me," Harris paused for a second, my eyes trained onto the ground as I let his words settle over me. "At first, I'd try to talk some sense into him, I would try to help him understand, this was my brother. But, one evening, my sister, Florence, came home with tear smeared across her cheeks, her lips bruised and busted, shaking with actual fear."

He inhaled sharply, I noticed how he closed his eyes but didn't comment on it.

"I was so confused; I didn't understand what happened. She didn't want to speak about it. Days turned into weeks, weeks turned into months, Flo wasn't this lively, happy person anymore, all that was a shell of herself. Then, I had brought Elijah over to chill, it had been a while since we did something like that because he'd always brush it off and say he was busy but finally I was able to convince him. At the same time, my sister was home and—"

Harris sniffed, I knew he was crying, and I didn't know what to do. My heart broke and I wanted to comfort, to offer him peace but I remained standing behind him like a statue. His cries were silent, his shoulders moving up and down. After a minute or two, he released a shaky breath of air.

"Damn it," he cursed under his breath before running his hands over his face, and then his fingers through his hair. "Florence came down the stairs and froze, her entire body stilled when she saw him. The colour on her face whitened as if she had seen a ghost and silent tears rolled down her cheeks. I was so confused, so lost. But Elijah wasn't. He knew exactly why she was crying."

I knew exactly where this was going, he didn't even need to say it and that's what killed me even more. My jaw clenched, my body ranging with pure anger and hatred that I felt like I couldn't breathe, that I was about to explode. The anger was so intense, so powerful, so violent.

"Harris—"

He interrupted me, facing me with a tear–stricken face, "He assaulted her, Candace. She was only fourteen, damn it! She trusted him as much as she trusted me, and he betrayed her. He took her right to say 'no' away. Like she was nothing. I let that bastard in my home. She was having nightmares about him and here I was, letting this monster into our home."

"You didn't know, Harris. You can't blame yourself," I insisted, shaking my head, suddenly aware of the tears on my cheeks.

"I couldn't protect her," His words were a whisper, a scar that wouldn't disappear. He closed his eyes, holding back his tears. "Just like I couldn't protect Scarlett."

-

So Elijah...

- fariha.

11 | phasma

C hapter XI: Phasma

Why is Elijah quiet all the time? Whenever I'd come to the table, he would immediately stop speaking and study me carefully, as if I was this difficult equation. He never once said a word to me since sitting with the Elites, I don't think I've ever heard him speak a full sentence when I was around. You also never spoke much about him; I don't understand why.

Winter Formal is coming around. I know you don't like to talk about it. It's interesting seeing how the pupils in Harrington prepare for the function, you never talked much about it. Don't worry, I don't intend on going. I don't know how long I can be around them, Scar. It's exhausting, I'm not as strong as you.

Sent by Candace at 8:00 A.M.

***

MY MOTHER WOULD tell me about the monsters that would hide in the dark. She would tell me to be careful, to trust no-one and that even those dear to you could betray your trust. People were selfish and evil, they lusted after supremacy. It was addictive, like a drug: the more that got within your system, the more you craved the twisted high.

Humanity was questionable. And Elijah was a clear example of that.

Harris didn't speak, his head down casted and shoulder slumping as if they held a vast amount of weight. It was most likely the guilt. No matter what he was told, he was always going to blame himself for the cause of Florence's situation. I understood that feeling, I felt it almost every day since Scarlett. We sat quietly around an empty table, far from the view of any curious onlookers, basking in the melancholy silence, my words stuck in my throat, my tongue felt restricted as if it was being held down and fatigue overwhelmed me.

It was burdensome to speak; I was in a loss of words because I didn't know what to say. My heart cried for Florence, she was too young to be forced to grow up quickly, she didn't deserve this. I sighed, running my hand over my face.

"Is she okay?" I winced once those words tumbled out of my mouth. Of course, she wasn't okay. What a stupid question to ask.

Inhaling sharply, he shrugged. "Some days, I see her smiling like her old self, but I know she cries herself to sleep. It's been a year and I know she still hasn't moved past it. I mean, how could she?"

"Does she still attend Harrington?"

He shook his head. "My parents pulled her out, they were adamant at first to keep her home-schooled, but I knew that would only make things worse. Florence was actually the one to suggest moving to Canada were our relatives lived. She's been there since."

"I'm sorry, Harris. She didn't deserve that, no one does," I mumbled, his eyes flickered over to me. "Did you tell someone?"

Instead of answering, Harris asked me, "Who is he, Candace?"

I frowned in confusion. "Elijah Astor."

"Exactly. Elijah Astor, the only son of Mr Astor, one of New York's top lawyers. A merciless man, a man that could even find a victim guilty. And Elijah was his son," Harris chuckled cynically, an underlying tone of pain lingering, mirroring how he was feeling within. "You don't think we tried to tell the police, to report it? Mr Astor couldn't have anyone ruin his or his son's reputation. Imagine that, a man fighting for justice has a son who sexually assaulted young girls. He'd be a joke."

I sucked in a sharp breath of air. Something Harris said caught my attention. Girls. Which meant Florence wasn't the only victim to Elijah's actions, that there were other girls who faced the same situation, who were also stripped away their right to say 'no'.

"In this city, money means power and power means you can have everything – even someone's silence," Harris sighed and left a deafening silence suffocating us. Then he spoke again, "Flo wasn't the only girl, he did it to so many others, but their cries were silenced, they were forgotten. Scarlett was one of them."

My heart stopped as my head snapped over to him, "What did you say?"

Harris slowly looked up at me. "It happened to Scarlett too."

My blood ran cold, my body suddenly felt weak as the lack of oxygen took its effect. I swallowed, tears immediately pricked my eyes and I clenched my fists, my hands paling as I constricted the blood flow to my fingers. This sudden wave of agony hit me, and I pursed my lips, squinting to fight back the tears that were threatening to escape. My heart hurt. It felt like I was getting stabbed and there was just so much pain, so much that it was becoming unbearable. I slacked against the wooden chair.

"When?"

"I thought you knew, Candace," he murmured, eyes glancing away from me, his shaggy hair shielding them from my piercing glare. "I'm sorry. This is not how you should've found out. I'm so sorry."

"When?" I gritted out.

"Beginning of summer, at some party."

Memories shifted through my mind until it came to a particular one.

Scarlett stood in the airport, shades covering her cloudy grey eyes, as she tapped on her phone with interest. Her red lips were arched into frown before lifting up as if she'd seen something humorous. Her auburn hair cascaded past her waist in elegant curls and she wore this white dress that made her look like an angel. I was in awe of her beauty. Compared to her, I was nothing.

She could've been passed off as a model and bystanders around her seemed to think so as well. Girls greeted her shyly, gushing her with compliments which Scarlett took politely, laughing melodically as some of them stumbled with their words. A few boys made a move on her and, although she was flattered, she respectfully declined them.

Jealousy nibbled within me as I observed the interaction; I struggled against it, reminding myself of my place. I studied her from the distance, noting that there was a change but when I greeted her, I didn't comment on it.

"Why the sudden visit?" I asked as we got into the car waiting outside for us.

She shrugged as she lifted her shades onto her head, "Can't I visit my best friend without a reason?"

"I mean, sure but you didn't even tell me until you landed this morning."

Scarlett scrutinized me before rolling her eyes. "I can always go if I'm not welcomed."

"Again, that's not what I'm saying," I sighed. There was no winning with her. An awkward tension suffocated us, it made me uncomfortable because it was unusual. Eventually, it broke when Scarlett kissed her teeth, running her manicured fingers through her lush hair as if this was a shampoo campaign.

"I'm avoiding some people."

I glanced over at her, a small smirk on my lips as I raised a brow. "Boy trouble?"

I didn't notice how her face paled slightly, the smile she gave me looked lost and meaningless, her body tensed up and her eyes filled with anguish and misery. I should've seen it. I was her best friend: the only person who knew her better than she knew herself. But I completely bypassed the change in character, ignoring it and played it off as if it was just another one of her attitudes due to being around the Elites for so long.

She looked away. "Something like that."

I blinked, the memory disappearing, "What else do you know?"

He sighed, running his fingers through his hair. "Scarlett was doing this documentary, I didn't understand why but she asked me to help, record the Elites whenever possible. She was always vague about what it was and never gave a full picture on what it was about, but I have no doubt it was to expose the Elites. I believe it was on her laptop, I think it's still at her house."

"In England?"

Shaking his head, he answered, "No, here. Her mother never sold that house after she moved back to England, I'm pretty sure a key is still hidden in the plant pot."

I was quiet, processing this new information whilst trying to calm down my emotions, I couldn't let them get the best of me. I promised to help Scarlett and that's what I intended to do. Standing up, I grabbed my bag and slipped it onto my shoulder, Harris's hesitant blue discs watching me. I didn't bother say bye, having a tunnel vision where I only saw red. I moved but I didn't even realise until Harris spoke from behind me.

"Where are you going?"

My answer was almost immediate.

"To take them down."

*

Wanting to cry has never felt so intense until today. I don't think I ever wanted to cry as much as I did right now. But, I refused to. Even if the emotion was so dominant and I could feel my muscles quivering, all strength lost, I still did not shed a tear. The closer it got to the Winter Formal, the more the urge to cry became stronger.

The days went by like a blur, I didn't even recognise myself some days, and the voices around me quietened until there was nothing. Loneliness easily became my new friend, I welcomed it with open arms. Some nights, I'd walk around aimlessly in my empty household; I cursed my mother for buying a house too big for a family of two. She was rarely home and if she was, she'd be sleeping but other than that, I seldom saw her, speaking less than four sentences to each other. She was busy with work and I was busy with taking the Elites down.

Today was one of those days. I sighed, grabbing the things out my locker on the day of the Winter Formal, when Zane strolled towards me, his hands tucked in his pocket as he occasionally greeted those in the corridor. He looked gorgeous as always, his dark hair was neatly combed back into a flick as if it was a comma, grey eyes hooded under thick lashes complemented by the dark and broody look he had going on.

My heart clenched. I had been avoiding him for some time, I knew he planned on asking me to the Winter Formal, but I had no intention of going, let along saying yes. Although, a relatively huge part of me wanted to go, I knew that I couldn't bring myself. I was a coward.

"Zane," I greeted.

"Where have you been, Candace? It's been a while and you're not answering my calls or messages," he frowned, concern laced in his voice. "Is everything okay?"

"Yes," I answered too quickly, catching him by surprise. "I mean, everything is okay. My mum hasn't been coming home lately and school is stressful. I got a lot on my plate."

There was little spark in his cloudy eyes, a small smile crawling onto his face as he crossed his arms over his chest, raising a brow and instantly I knew what he was about to do.

"You should give yourself a break, stop overworking yourself," Don't ask, don't ask, don't ask. "You should come to the Winter Formal? With me?"

Damn it.

I exhaled. "I can't. I plan on going back to England for Christmas and I haven't packed yet. I'm sorry."

My lie was lousy, stupid and highly unbelievable, but it was all I could think of it that moment. Giving him a sad smile, his face dropped, and cheeks burned as he scratched the back of his neck, looking anywhere other than at me. Guilt greeted me and I basked in it, pursing my lips together as held back the urge to comfort him.

"Oh! Right, well.... I'll see you around?"

Nodding softly, I said, "I'll see you around. Have a good holiday, Zane."

Quickly composing himself, he gave me his famous smirk and winked. "It won't be fun without you."

After seeing me roll my eyes, he laughed, throwing his head back before walking away, catching up with Elijah and Kaito, who were waiting for him in the distance. I hugged my books closely, observing the three members of the Elites as they spoke amicably to each other, knowing full well of the secrets they have hidden from public eye. Secrets I intended to expose.

"You're really not going?" I heard someone say behind me, causing me to jump in surprise. I sent a glare to Harris over my shoulder, who returned an embarrassed grin back.

"No. Can we leave now?" I insisted. "We don't have much time left."

He rolled his eyes. "So demanding."

That evening, whilst everyone attended the Winter Formal, an occasion celebrated at the end of the semester in a beautiful hotel under a diamond chandelier, financed by Harrington Industries, I stood outside the Lockwood's household, a large mansion (not as big as Celeste's) but large enough considering her father was an engineer. After finding the key hidden in one of the plant pots that Harris mentioned, my hand wavered over the door handle, apprehensively contemplating whether I want to enter or not.

"I'll stay outside," Harris muttered. "Take your time."

Although I heard him speak, within seconds I forgot what he had said. Nevertheless, I nodded before gulping as I turned the handle. The house was eerily desolate, the lights switched off, coldness seeping into rooms as if it was scene from a horror movie. After finding the lights switch, with ease, I trekked around the house, softly touching the dusty photo frames that remained on the shelves besides the vase of dead flowers, petals shrivelled up and lost its colour.

My breathing was shaky, my body was aching from exhaustion, crying to me to rest but I didn't. I continued to investigate the downstairs before slowly climbing up the marble stairs. The last room at the end of the corridor, I kept repeating in my head, my heart thumping as if it was about to exploded from my chest.

Every step I took was a step I wish I didn't take. My senses became heightened in this environment, it almost felt like I was hiding from a murderer, as I cautiously moved down the corridor, photos hanging on the wall haunting me as they were illuminated by the moonlight that gleamed through the oval window behind me.

I was shaking but it was hard to tell whether it was from the cold or anxiety. Eventually, I stood in front of her bedroom, hesitating on whether I wanted to do this or not, if I was ready to see the truth, the secrets that she kept hidden from me.

I exhaled unevenly as I grabbed the cold metal knob, and turned it, hearing a creaky sound as the door opened to reveal Scarlett's bedroom. Flicking the light switch on, florescent lights illuminated the rose coloured room, silk sheets covered the bed, her drawer left untouched, work scattered across her desk remained unfinished, the scent of her favourite perfume still lingered in the air; her presence so strong that I thought she was right next to me.

Mustering up all the courage I had left in me, I decided to not spend too much time in here and to focus at the task at hand. Quickly, I searched through her wardrobe where her designer clothes hung, any drawer around the room, her vanity, inside the cupboard in her bathroom, her desk before I finally gave up. My mind came to a blank as I thought hard on where she'd keep it but, as if someone was sending a sign, something glittered underneath her bed as the moonshine peaked through the cracks of the closed linen curtains.

I frowned as I bent down, retrieving a silver laptop from underneath the shopping bags under her bed, a small gasp escaping my lips. I found it. I actually found it. A part of me was relieved whilst the other dreaded the answers I would find. And, in the far back of a mind, a questioned lingered: Did she find something on Zane?

I hated how I prayed for him to innocent and that I was setting myself up for heartbreak. I guess that's what Scarlett meant when she called him a teenage dream. Tears pricked my eyes once again as I finally focused my attention on the room, loss of words and filled with so much pain. It was insufferable. There weren't enough words to describe that pain I was in, like someone had ripped my heart out.

I pressed my lips, standing up to leave when I noticed the beautiful girl with auburn hair leaning against the doorway, her skin pale like porcelain and was illuminated by the moonlight that beamed from behind her, her grey eyes twinkled with life and mischief, Prada's giving her extra height and complementing the stunning navy dress that had diamonds scattered across her waist like a belt and fell just above her knees.

My heart stopped.

"Hey, Candy," she smirked. "Missed me?"

I froze for a brief second. Then, I screamed.

I don't know how long I screamed or how loud I was, I didn't even realise when Harris rushed into the room, his eyes wide with worry when he spotted me on the floor with the laptop clutched against my chest, my throat sore from screaming yet I didn't stop. He immediately came to my aid, bringing me into the safety of his arms, rocking me like a child as I clasped tightly onto his shirt, cooing me with words of comfort.

"Candace, there's nothing here. There's nothing here," he hushed, pulling me closer to his hold. "There's nothing here."

It was only then when I noticed my face stained with tears, tears I had been holding for weeks, tears that revealed the torment raging within me, tears of heartbreak. They kept rolling down my cheeks, ruining his shirt but he wasn't bothered as he continued to whisper words of solace to me, and I clung onto those words to find some sense of peace but alas, nothing helped repair how broken I truly was – nothing to mask how broken I was, not even makeup and designer clothes.

I eventually peeked over his shoulder, sniffling and hiccupping my cries, and noticed the ethereal redhead saunter down the corridor, glancing over her shoulder as she sent me a smirk and a wink, before disappearing into the moonlight.

Scarlett.

-

Thoughts on Scarlett?

Part one is complete. Part two will begin on Sunday.

- fariha.

PART 2

I^{mperium}

□A large chair does not make a king.□

[Sudanese Proverb]

power

fariha.

12 | last straw

Chapter XII: Last Straw

Candace, why aren't you replying to my messages? I haven't spoken to you at all during the winter holidays. You didn't even message me during Christmas, our favourite festive event. What's going on? It's not like you to ignore me for so long.

What happened?

Hello?

Candace?

Sent by Scarlett at 2:00 A.M.

***

SOMETIMES, NUMB WASN'T the right word to use to describe how one was feeling. The winter was especially chilly this year; snow leisurely blanketing the New York roads and skyscrapers until it looked like a scene

out from Winter Wonderland. Yet, I felt no joy towards the winter festiv-
ities.

I felt nothing.

Everything moved around me slowly like time had stopped, like the world
had come to a standstill and I was the only one breathing. Although, it
didn't feel like I was breathing. My mind raced with thousands of thoughts,
my emotions trapped and caged far within me but, my body was running
in slow motion. The grief and sadness weighed heavily on my shoulders, I
constantly felt tired and spent most of my time hidden under the comfort
of my bed sheets. Everything hurt. It hurt so much.

I just wanted it to go away.

I didn't realise how quickly time went, not that I cared. Christmas came
and went, and soon did the New Year, entering us into a new season,
another fresh start, yet, it felt as if I was reliving the same days over and over
again. My heart cried in agony, telling me to stop, to stop hurting myself
but I refused to listen, to understand, to stop letting myself be in pain.

I used that anger and pain to fuel my urge to complete what I came to do.
Every day, every moment, every second, I spent thoroughly calculating my
plan out and, not for one second did I forget who I was doing this for.
Some days, I would catch a glimpse of myself in the mirror and I wouldn't
recognise the person staring back at me.

She looked so hollow, so lost. Her eyes had dark circles underneath them,
her eyes were so distant, they blurred with tears, her face pale like a ghost
and her body slugged with sorrow. Everything was nothing and nothing
was everything.

"Candace," A soft whisper caressed my cheeks. "Sweetie."

I refused to open my eyes, to see the concern in my mother's eyes, to see the damage I had caused. So, I kept my eyes closed, holding back the tears that threatened to expose my innermost feelings, clenching my jaw when I heard her sigh sadly, her gentle fingertips brushing the lone hair strand away from my face before she lightly kissed the top of my head.

She hovered around for a few more minutes before deciding to leave, the doors closing behind her just as the waterworks started. Blinking my eyes open, the sun blinded me as it peaked through the cracks of the curtain, a shiver crawling up my spine as I was greeted with a cold presence sitting at the end of my bed.

Her hair was particularly red today, especially as the sun spotlighted her, accentuating her radiance. Her grey, almond shaped eyes stared into the distance as she silently sat, her lips painted in the iconic red, dressed in black dress that stopped just above her knees and her lucky heels finalising the look.

"When will this be over?" she asked as I sat up, running my hands through my tangled hair.

"I don't know."

"I can't stay forever," Her attention shifted to the picture on top of my vanity, there was a ghost of a smile on her face. "I'm going to leave soon."

"I know," I breathed out softly, closing my eyes.

She didn't say anything, but I felt her shift closer to me, her porcelain hands rested on top of mine, cold and icy. It almost made me flinch, but her steely grey eyes held me in captivity when I looked up and all thoughts dispersed instantly. It was just me and her.

That's all that mattered.

"I love you, Candace," she said. "Always."

The corner of my lips quirked up. "I love you too."

*

The first day back always gave me butterflies in my stomach, thoughts running aimlessly in my mind, doubts questioning my judgement as I greeted people in the hallway on my way to the cafeteria.

What if the Elites forgot who I am? What if they found who I am? What if they found out my plan? There were too many what ifs which caused an unsettled feeling to rest in my stomach, making me nauseous. Not only were the Elites making me nervous but during the winter holidays, I also received offers from Harvard University and Oxford University, two of the top universities that I have dreamt of attending since I was little girl.

It only made sense for me to attend the universities that my parents went to hence why I made sure that I excelled in everything I did, whilst maintain a good reputation and background. If I was to tell the Elites about these offers, I had no doubt that once the effects of my plan take place they'll rest at nothing until they ruined all possible gateways to me having a successful future.

That's why I lied.

"Brown," I answered, situating myself in the haunted eighth seat, when Akari asked if I had any offers.

Her eyes lit up as she grinned at. "That's great!"

Celeste shrugged with a bored expression. "It's alright."

Akari rolled her eyes. "I think that's great."

"What about you guys?" I asked, diverting the attention to someone other than me.

"Elijah got in Cornell," Akari said cheerfully, his names sending unpleasant shivers down my spine.

I swallowed my disgust as I squinted at Elijah, who silently observed the conversation. His hazel eyes were hidden under his shaggy strawberry blonde hair, but they held dark intentions — secrets and skeletons that deserved to be shown to the world.

"Congrats," I said, holding back the bitterness.

He nodded. "Thanks."

"I heard you both are going Yale," Zane commented, looking at the Ice King and Queen. Celeste bobbed, planting a kiss on her boyfriend's cheek, his arm resting around her shoulder, squeezing her in his hold. "I didn't realise you wanted to go Yale, Celeste."

Her jaw clenched as her taciturn eyes snapped over to him, narrowing until they looked like blades. "It was mutual decision. He's my future and I'm his."

"Of course," Zane agreed but there was an underlying tone of sarcasm that was hard to miss. It pissed Celeste off, a scowl on her lips, but Bentley looked amused as there was a trace of a smile threatening to escape.

Noticing the strain, Madeline quickly jumped in, her blue eyes concentrating onto Zane. "You got into Columbia? Mr Harrington mentioned it during the holidays."

"Oh, yes. Father said you got into Columbia. You must be excited to go to the same university as your father, I bet he's proud."

Bentley's word held a great amount of mockery and insincerity, if Zane heard it, he didn't show. Instead, he nodded with a smile, but his eyes spoke differently. Kaito was like a hyena, jumping to the chance to make a snide comment, his eyes twinkled with malicious intent.

"Not surprising at all," Kaito chuckled bitterly. "A slip of money makes bad boy good."

Zane's eyes suddenly flared in anger, his jaw tightening as he curled his fist, glaring at the Japanese boy who sat opposite him. The abrupt mood shocked me, my eyes drawing together as I looked at him in confusion. Not only what Kaito said upset Zane but Bentley clearly disapproved of it as his eyes creased, shaking his head as he kissed his teeth.

"Kaito, do you need another reminder of your place?" Bentley threatened which caused Kaito to scowl, looking away with his arms crossed over his chest. Zane still looked guarded and livid which made Akari uncomfortable, so, she quickly changed the focus, her eyes brightening as she sat up straighter.

"Kaito and I plan on heading back to Japan to continue our studies," Akari stated, playfully nudging her twin brother, who gave a smile only reserved for her. "It was a difficult decision but we both agreed that I could further purse my musical career, especially if my father can personally mentor me, and Kaito will learn the ropes of the business in order to take over once Dad retires."

"Which is never," Kaito snorted, his sister giving him a disapproving look, a small sulk on her face which caused him to sigh, muttering a quiet apology. Immediately, her mood brightened up, twisting her hands around his arm. I noticed how his gaze softened as she began to amicably talk about how excited she was to travel back home, his body posture relaxed, and his attention was solely on her.

"I didn't apply for any universities," Madeline exclaimed, cutting off Akari from her rant, popping a grape into her mouth, eyes shifting their concentration onto the blonde bombshell.

"I thought you planned on going to Columbia because that's where your new beau was going and you're being forced to," Zane questioned with a raised brow, looking slightly less angry.

"It didn't work out."

I was surprised when I saw how everyone acted indifferently towards the latest news, but quickly dismissed it when I remembered this was Madeline that we were talking about. I sipped on my coffee, glancing at Akari who gave me a smirk before wiping it off as she ate her chips.

"So, what happened?" Akari asked nonchalantly.

"He chickened out," Madeline shrugged. "Something about too many risks. I don't know, I don't really care. It's just annoying and sets me back."

I frowned, cocking my head to the side. "What do you mean?"

Madeline glanced at me, her blue eyes thinning as they scrutinized at me for a good amount of time before Bentley chuckled, my attention shifting onto him, and was about to reply when Celeste coughed, clamping her jaw. He peered down at his significant other, the pair sending eye messages, before he sighed, rolling his russet discs in amusement. Of course, they still didn't trust me, and I don't blame them. what they'll never know is that I knew the answer, I was the cause of her broken relationship, but this interaction just confirmed what I needed to hear.

I'll never be a part of them.

*

"Are you attending the banquet that Zane's father is holding this evening?" Akari asked after school.

She looked cute dressed in a red coat that reminded me of Little Red Riding Hood, her hair was braided yet, it still reached below her waist. Although the weather was chilly, she wore a plaid skirt and a white blouse adorned by the crystal, necktie brooch with a red and black ribbon attached to it.

The coat was the only clothing that kept her warm; she didn't even have black tights, like me, that enclosed warmth. Nevertheless, she wore a stunning smile as she glanced at me, arm curled around mine, not looking the slightest bit bothered by the icy weather.

"I'm not sure, I'm really behind in work," I lied.

She sighed. "Come on, it's the first event of the year. You can't not go."

There was a little pout on her face as she gave me puppy dog eyes, tugging on my arm as I avoided her gaze. She whined when I wasn't paying an attention to her; she was only amusing me further. Eventually, I gave into her demands which earned me a little squeal as she jumped in happiness, hugging me tightly that she nearly cut off all my oxygen supply.

"I... can't... breathe," I gasped out. Giggling, she let go of me with a sheepish grin on her face, biting her lower lip as she watched me hunch over, trying to inhale as much air as I could.

"Sorry."

I glowered at her.

That evening, with the help of Akari, I wore a scarlet evening gown that cinched around my waist, the silk material tangled around my neck as the dress was backless, dipping far too down to my liking but, Akari argued otherwise and stated that it was sophisticated yet risky — like me. I frowned and wanted to ask what she meant, but she quickly cut the call, after informing me that she'd be leaving soon. The event, hosted by the Strykers, was to commemorate their children's entry to their desired universities — at least that's what I was told by Zane when he invited me, but I knew otherwise.

The purpose of the event to scout out new business partners and root out the weeds in their community. Akari didn't even need to confirm my thoughts on whether the Harrington's were involved in the event or not, I knew full well that they were. In order to control your people, you must give the slightest bit of power to those below you so that once you take it away, they'll be coming back for more.

It's funny how power was so similar to a drug. The high, it's addictiveness, the adrenaline; having power gave it all to you, and the Harrington's favourite part of power was taking it away. Now, you were left with withdrawal and that's the most dangerous part. It left you weak and easily manipulated, hence why the Strykers were doing the dirty work which should've been in the hands of Mr Harrington.

Their household was unreasonably large — although, nothing could outcompete with Celeste's house. Cars of all different brands and types ranked both sides once you drove past the barred gates. People flooded into the house, reporters capturing their pictures and flashing lights blinding me when my car parked in front of the steps.

I braced myself for what was to come when the door opened, maintaining as smile as my driver helped me out — nevertheless, I was rather uncomfortable with reporters throwing questions in my face regarding tonight's event. As much as I wanted to roll my eyes, I couldn't. Zane told me this would be a quiet gathering but, from the look of it, one would've thought that a celebrity had arrived.

My hair was styled into a bun, loose curls cascading onto my shoulders which bounced as I walked up the stairs, bunching my dress up at the front so I didn't embarrass myself by tripping. I caught my reflection in one of the camera lenses and quickly looked away, not recognising the girl with makeup on and her signature red lips, that looked especially gloomy today. I refused to acknowledge how empty I looked, how invested I was in destroying the Elites.

I just couldn't.

It didn't take me long to find Akari as she was wearing this magnificent purple dress that sparkled in glitter, complemented by a simple pearl neck-lace — a gift given by her mother. I wasted no time and moved towards her whilst adoring the interior of the home. It was warm, the essence of oak wood and red gave it an urbane and wealthy ambience.

There was a family portrait hanging above the fireplace — Zane wore a navy suit, his hair combed back, revealing his silvery eyes. His facial expression was rather stoic and stiff, similarly to his father, who was a splitting image of his son. He sat besides his wife, his second wife in fact, whilst Zane stood behind them, hands behind his back.

"Candace," Akari snapped me back to reality, my eyes flickering away from the portrait to her, a small crease on her forehead when she walked towards me, handing me a glass of wine. "Are you okay?"

"Yeah, sorry. I was about to come to you, but this caught my attention," I answered, pointing at the picture.

She glanced up. "Mrs Carmichael is truly a beauty, isn't she?"

"Oh, you flatter me, Akari dear," We jumped simultaneously when another voice spoke instead of mine.

Akari's eyes widened when she looked at me, shock covering her face. Hesitantly, I glanced over my shoulder just as Akari plastered on her brightest smile, holding her hand out towards Zane's stepmother. She was a beautiful brunette, tall with bright blue eyes that looked as deep as the ocean. There's was this smile, similar to the painting, like she knew something I did not. It was unnerving, but, lately, everything has made me uncomfortable like I was on the edge of a cliff.

She wore the most gorgeous, expensive gown that perfectly accentuated her figure, the deep purple complimented her eyes, her porcelain cheekbones were covered in blush, bringing colour to her face, and glitter which highlighted her astonishing features. She almost looked as if she was a painting.

"It's been a while, Miss Takahashi," Mrs Carmichael mused.

"I'm sorry that I haven't been able to visit," Akari replied before glancing at me. "Ma'am, this is Candance Lowell. She recently transferred to Harrington from England."

Mrs Carmichael's eyes widened slightly as she shifted her focus onto me, before she held her hand out towards me; my body racking with anxiety but I did my best not to show it. Her hands were soft yet had this firm hold, her nails neatly manicured and painted gold.

"I've heard much about you."

My eyes broadened in surprise. "You have?"

She laughed angelically. "Of course, my dear. From Zane."

Unnoticeably, I exhaled in relief. "All good things I hope."

"I suppose you've captured my son's heart, haven't you?" She teased, a spark in her eyes caused me to blush.

"Zane's practically in love with her," Akari joked, impishly bumping her shoulder into mine.

"That's not true," I grimaced.

Mrs Carmichael's smile widened like a Cheshire. "Just because you do not see it, does not mean that it's not true."

If possible, my heart stuttered as if it stumbled, trying to regain its regular pace. It never crossed my mind that Zane saw me that way but now that I knew that it was possible, guilt gnawed inside me. I didn't want to hurt him; he was the most honest man I knew, and I hated lying to him. The sadness within me quadrupled but I did my best not to show as I smiled alongside Akari when Mrs Carmichael spoke fondly about her son.

"Zane has a bright future ahead of him and I have no doubt that he won't disappoint," she said tenderly. "I do hope you'll be alongside, Miss Lowell. You seem like a lovely girl from what I've been told."

Words can deceive you.

"Please, call me Candace," I insisted.

The corner of her lips quirked further upwards, "Candace."

Although she was subtle, I spotted how her eyes analysed me as if she was memorising my features and expressions, before they met mine, the same spark in her eyes only lightened when she had noticed I had done the same thing. The moment was short–lived, but it wasn't hard to understand what had occurred.

"Candace," Someone called out, almost breathlessly. My attention wavered to the person behind Mrs Carmichael, who glanced over her shoulder. Zane, adorned in a black suit and tie, his chestnut hair was combed and gelled back into an undercut rather than its curly state which covered those misty grey eyes.

"Zane," His mother said. "So nice of you to finally join us."

Momentarily, his eyes moved onto his mother as he closed the distance between us, hesitantly watching her whilst simultaneously admiring me. From the corner of my eyes, I noticed Akari smirking before walking away with a quiet goodbye, my jaw clenching in annoyance.

"I had a call," he replied, vaguely, "I see that you've introduced yourself to each other."

His posture was tense, his shoulders squared back, jaw tightened, and eyes steadily observing his stepmother as he positioned himself by my side, startling me when his arm slipped around my waist and drew me to closer to his side. I looked up at him with wide eyes, unable to hide my astonishment, but he paid no attention to me. Mrs Carmichael smirked, gone the angelic features and replaced with mischief; one brow raised in delight as she crossed her arms over her chest.

"Don't be like that, Zane," she sighed. "It's only my right to meet your girlfriend."

Her word held revulsion, as if my presence affected her deeply, when I realised that it was all a façade and everything she had said before were worth nothing — they were just words. My heart sunk, my body unknowingly shrinking closer to Zane, his arm tightening around my waist protectively as he scowled at his stepmother.

" You don't have that right," he scoffed slipping his hand into mine, my breath hitching for a moment. "Just remember, you're only my mother by law."

Her eyes narrowed heatedly, her mouth opening to retort something back, but Zane didn't give her the last word as he dragged me away from someone I thought was the only decent person in this society. Guess I was wrong. Words can deceive you. I didn't even need to look at him to know he was furious — his grip hand tightened around mine as if he was afraid to let go and his posture was stiff like a statue.

We walked past the rest of our group, who gave us confused glances, but he didn't pay any attention to them as he led me to an empty room. Letting go of my hand, he slammed the door, the noise rocketing around the room, before pacing up and down. I watched him cautiously, unable to speak as my anxiety betrayed me — my mouth opening and closing like a fish.

"Why were you speaking to her?" he growled.

"Don't blame me, she came up to us. I was with Akari and we were speaking about your family portrait."

"That bloody family portrait," he grumbled. His finger ran through his hair as he came to a halt, his grey eyes glancing at me. "Don't speak to her for the rest of the night."

I frowned. "You can't tell me what to do."

"I can and you'll listen, Candace," Every syllable held a tremendous amount of power and warning. I flinched, stepping back, which caused his eyes to soften and his shoulders to relax as an agitated sigh shakily left his lips. "Please, Candace."

I didn't like the tension between us, it was choking me, and my heart heaved in hurt when I took in his pained expression, so I reluctantly nodded, looking away from him. There was a heavy silence between us before I heard his shoes tap against the wooden flooring as he stepped closer to me; one hand captured mine whilst the other gently caressed my cheek, my eyes nervously gazing up at him. There was this tender smile as he tugged me closer to him until there was barely a metre gap between us.

"Forgive my behaviour," he whispered before pausing as if he was trying to gather his words. "I... I care about you, Candace. My stepmother hasn't got your best interest at heart, she's playing her mind games and I can't let her hurt you. I won't let her. Just trust me, please."

I hated how my emotions got the best of me, how his words charmed me, how they fed me fake hope. I hate how my heart clung tightly onto every word said, how it swooned at his dashing features and secret promises. I hated it. More importantly, I hated him — or so I wished I did. Before I could even reply, the door opened and Bentley strolled in, one hand tucked in his pocket, the corner of his lips lifted up in a smirk when he took in the situation.

"Your father is calling you, Zane," he stated, eyes flickering to Zane and me, before he raised a brow. "Did I interrupt something?"

Zane's eyes didn't waver from mine for the longest time until Bentley called out his name, that was when he finally acknowledged his best friend's presence and released me from his captive after one final look. I didn't understand him, I didn't want to, but a huge part of me was filled with curiosity and wanted to venture further into Zane's past.

Information he was withheld from me was problem in my best interest, but, as he strode away alongside Bentley, closing the door behind him, my eyes immediately shifted to the first thing I noticed the second I came in the room. The ebony door in the far corner.

From the look of this room alone, the couches circled around a glass coffee table, the bookshelves and the dim lamps with plants in the corner of the room, I gathered this must be where Captain Stryker held his meetings and if my assumptions were correct, then the second door must lead to his office. My hand nervously gripped onto the knob and with a shaky breath, I opened the door — revealing a neat office that had a fireplace, the interior similar to the rest of the house with another family portrait, only this time another woman had taken the place of Mrs Carmichael.

Mrs Stryker.

She was stunningly blonde, her eyes grey with hints of green, her lips full of colour as she smiled from ear to ear. Unlike Mrs Carmichael, Mrs Stryker looked vivacious and full of life, her cheeks were rosy as she held onto her son in her arms, Captain Stryker standing impassively behind her, one hand on her shoulder. Zane looked no older than 6 months, cradled in his mother's arms whilst she sat, clearly being the light in the Stryker family.

I had no doubt that the loss of his mother whilst he was a kid was the reason he detested his stepmother, who entered his life as he entered adolescence. Closing my eyes momentarily, gathering my thoughts, I refused to allow my emotions betray me and my mission. Without another look at the portrait, I examined the room, looking through paperwork and cabinets, searching through files and drawers when something caught my eye.

Tucked underneath a pile of books in Captain Stryker's desk, the University of Columbia logo was poking out. Curiosity killed a cat, and the moment I took it out was a moment I wish didn't happen. My heart lurched when I read the words on the white paper, my faith in the person I had given at least a bit of my trust diminished with every sentence.

Captain Stryker,

Your generous donation will be in good use for our students' education. Thank you for all the help in regenerating our University to ensure the best possible education and experience for our students.

Regarding your concern, you should no longer worry about it as it will be handled confidentially, and your donation will remain known as anonymous.

Zane will be ensured a spot in Columbia; this interaction will remain undisclosed to the public as requested. I hope you have a wonderful Christmas, wishing you the best and I look forward to seeing your son next fall.

Yours Sincerely, Principal Hamilton.

University of Columbia.

My hand shook and I felt a lone tear rolling down my cheeks. Betrayal and regret clenched tightly against my heart; for a second, it felt like I couldn't breathe. Without another thought, I quickly tucked the letter back into its original position, doing a swift scout, before quietly leaving the room. Marching past the living room, I heard Zane's laughter in the distance, my eyes flicking over in his direction.

His eyes crinkled up as he grinned from ear to ear at something his friends had said, clinking his glass against Kaito's. In that moment, I felt nothing. I didn't hesitate to send him a quick text — a lie — about why I left early, before dashing down the stairs where my town car was waiting for me. Even then, I felt nothing. Why did it hurt so much? What else could I expect from an Elite? That's what he was — an Elite.

I got so lost in his seductive words and teasing smiles that I forgot who he was. Of course, he'd cheat his way into an Ivy League. Of course, everything was handed to him on a silver platter. Of course, he lied about it. The biggest joke of it all was that he expected me to trust him — and I nearly did.

I didn't bother greeting my mother, who quietly sat in the living room, working, as I bolted up the stairs, wanting to desperately get this gown off me. This façade, this illusion, the lies. I couldn't even look at my reflection, I didn't want to know who I'd see... I don't think I would recognise her. I collapsed onto my bed, closing my eyes as silent tears spilt onto my cheek. That's when I felt the pain — pure torment.

I choked back my sobs when I heard my phone vibrate on my phone: his name blinking repeatedly. I didn't answer. Instead, I tucked the phone underneath my pillow and drew out the laptop from within my bedside table. Trembling, I opened the screen, holding my breath as the device started up, fighting back my anxiety. Besides me, she quietly sat before cocking her head to the side, a sad look on her face, her hands knotted together.

"Are you sure you want to do this?" she whispered; shivers crawled down my spine.

"No," I replied as I typed in her password — the year she was born.

The screen lit up, greeting me with her home page, a slide show of pictures as her background. Coincidently, a picture of us hugging came up and my heart shattered.

"Why are you doing this?"

I didn't look in her direction as I scoured through her files until I found the one I'd been looking for. The one that would reveal everything. The secrets, the lies, the plots and plans. The whole lot. And I don't know I was ready for it.

"Because I'm done with the Elites," I answered, clicking the video. The video expanded until it covered the entire screen, a black screen welcomed me.

I held my breath.

A second later, a girl with auburn hair appeared, seating herself in front of the camera, her eyes wild and lost, her cheeks pale, her red lips smiling.

"Hi, I'm Scarlett Lockwood."

-

Well then...

- fariha.

13 | scarlett's eyes

C hapter XIII: Scarlett's Eyes

I'm sorry.

Sent by Scarlett at 12:00 P.M.

***

November 2017.

"Are you recording?" Scarlett asked, pouting whilst Harris focused the camera on her.

"Yes," he replied from behind the camera. "You can start."

The pout morphed into a bright smile as she flicked her hair behind her shoulders. Her eyes creased when she smiled, her cheeks rosy and her lips painted red. They sat in Scarlett's room, the sunlight beaming through the window and onto Scarlett as if it was her personal spotlight.

"To the students of Harrington Preparatory," she began. "I'm here to reveal the truth behind the Elites."

She walked towards her couch, settling the down as the camera followed her. Although, she looked confident, Scarlett was actually shaking inside — afraid of the unknow, afraid of what will happen next. But, she had come so far that she was too far gone to go back. She had devoted most of her high school life on bringing the Elites down and she wasn't going to stop anytime soon.

Her grey eyes momentarily flickered over to the frame that rested on her vanity; encased was a picture of her and Candace with grin plastered across their face, drenched from head to toe from the water pistols.

"You must think that there are these esteemed, beautiful people, could do no wrong. Well, I beg to differ. The Elites are a very private group of friends, to be one you must catch their attention," she paused fleetingly. "I caught their attention. I jumped from the third clique to the top in less than a couple of months. On their table was the eighth seat that many people wanted because you could have power, but for the Elites, you were just another pawn. They played with you, toyed with your emotions, get you high on the glitz and glam until you wanted more. Not to brag, but I held the longest record of sitting in that seat. It's been nearly 2 years since I joined the Elites and let me tell you something, they never accepted me as one of their own."

She released a bitter laugh, her eyes downcasted before she regained her composure, a saccharine smile on her lips.

"Like I said, a private group of friends. You can sit with them, party with them, gossip with them and rule with them, but you'll never be them. But, even the Elites have weakness within the group. Secretly, they all despised one another; they've all hurt one another but acted to each other's face as if nothing happened. Imagine attending parties after parties, watching them do the most terrible things to each other and then, at lunch the next day, they'd smile and laugh as if nothing happened. I guess, that's what happens when you've been friends for too long - sorry isn't in their vocabulary, I'm pretty sure it doesn't even exist to them.

"The Elites were a complex group, friends whose best interest wasn't for each other but for themselves. See, they were strong as a group law bricks to a building, but if one brick falls - the rest soon falls afterwards. Now, don't get me wrong, this documentary isn't a vengeance thing, it's more of me enlightening my fellow students about the wrong and repulsive things the Elites have done and gotten away with," Standing up, she neatly brushed down her skirt before looking dead straight into the camera. "Once I'm done, you'll never bow to the Elites again."

*

September 2017.

"Is it on?" she asked, the location changing to the Harrington cafeteria.

Her and Harris sat on the mezzanine, just above where the Elites sat and far enough so that any onlookers would not catch a glimpse of what they were doing. Harris nodded and Scarlett grinned; the uniform she wore slightly different to everyone else. Her blouse was far more fitted than the average student, and her skirt was hiked up high that it just fell mid-thigh. She wore stockings and her favourite pair of heels, her hair neatly combed back into a ponytail and her makeup enhancing her features. The camera captured her beauty.

"Today is the first day back at Harrington and that means it's time to fish out the weak spots in our little society," Scarlett informed. "It's the Elites favourite pastime. Unfortunately, I can't bring Harris down to the table but from this view up here, he'll be able to capture everything like a bird."

She lifted a brow as a smirk crossed her face, her hands clasping together, her eyes filled with hateful intent. Her intentions were nothing pure, her hatred was strong and empowering, it engulfed her, it was the reason she sat with them that lunch.

"How was your summer, Scar?" Akari asked, greeting her with a hug as the redheaded settled besides her.

"Nothing of any excitement, though I did go back to England. My closest friend lives there and I decided to pay her a visit," Scarlett replied, pushing a strand of loose hair behind her ear. "How was Japan? You left early during the summer; I didn't even get to say bye."

"I knew you missed me despite saying otherwise," Akari grinned when Scarlet gave a deadpan look. "It was great. We didn't see much of dad. Not surprised."

Scarlett gave her a frown. "You spent your time there with just your mother?"

"Most the time. Although, Kaito spent majority of his time out the house," This time, Akari frowned. "I wonder where he went off to."

Although, she shrugged it off as if it was nothing, Scarlett knew otherwise.

The scene changed — Scarlett sat in front of the camera with a concentrated look on her face, her brows creasing as she frowned.

"Akari had no clue what Kaito was actually doing in Japan, why he actually wanted to go back home," she said. "See, our Takahashi boy was in the drug business which isn't all that surprising but that was just a side project. No, the real business was the illegal dealing of artefacts stolen from China and Japan."

In front of her sat five files — files which had the evidence to contradict an argument used to defend the Elites. She was prepared, she knew what she was doing and even if it costed her life, she didn't care. Slowly, she revealed images of Kaito in different locations — at his warehouse, bags of drugs, in Japan, the artefacts, the paperwork. Especially, the image of him dealing drugs to the youngers of Harrington — she had everything. Enough to send him to jail for a very, very long time, and damage the Takahashi name — and Scarlett had the intention to do so.

"Kaito," Scarlett smirked. "Did you think no one would find out?"

The scene flickered back to the cafeteria, Harris carefully recording all Elites' interactions. Scarlett was talking to Akari when her brother, Madeline and Zane strolled in as if it was a runway, capturing the eyes of the students sitting around them. Madeline smirked when she saw Kaito wink at his fangirls whilst Zane rolled his eyes in disinterest.

However, when he saw Scarlett, he perked up, straightening his spine as he greeted her with a beam. The interaction between Zane and Scarlett seemed too private that the camera recording them felt like it was evading their personal space. Her eyes lit up and the corner of her lips reached her eyes as she grinned when his arms rested around her shoulder as he sat down.

"Lockwood," he greeted, pinching her chips. "Haven't seen you all this summer."

"She went abroad," Akari chided in, striking Madeline's curiosity, her blue eyes focusing away from her phone, beadily staring Scarlett down.

"Where did you go?" she asked, raising a brow.

"England," Scarlett answered, challenging Madeline's gaze. As if she was surrendering, Madeline nodded slowly before leaning back in her seat, sipping on her latte as she refocused her attention onto her phone.

"Who's in England?" Kaito snorted.

"My best friend. I'd love for you guys to meet her one day."

From the way Zane's lips curled, Scarlett knew he was about to say something flirty. "Is she cuter than you?:

With a roll of her eyes, she slapped his hand away her chips. "Much cuter. Not your type."

He raised a brow. "Didn't know I had a type."

They held each other's gaze as if they were testing each other, the air shifting between them when, from besides Scarlett, Akari pretended to throw up, gagging as she watched the interaction between her two friends, breaking the tension.

"Stop flirting, its suffocating."

Scarlett glowered as Zane laughed, releasing her from his captive. The 'friends' began to all inform one another about the events that occurred during the summer with little knowledge that Scarlett knew everything they'd been up to. So, when they lied to each other, she knew the truth behind it, the unspoken words.

The atmosphere quickly turned icy the second the doors opened and in strolled the rulers of Harrington. Scarlett didn't bat a lash their way, her focus remained on Akari as the Japanese girl did her best to not glance back. The girl with the auburn hair did her best to not smirk at Akari's reaction, threatening to expose her innermost feeling — especially as the couple sat opposite her.

"It's been a while," Bentley said, glancing at everyone but Akari, his eyes skimming over her — a flicker of hurt crossing her expression. "How's everyone been?"

"Madeline was just telling us about her latest expenditure," Kaito snorted.

"When he said expenditure, he was actually talking about her latest hook-up," Scarlett let out a low chuckle — bitter and amused all at the same time. "See, we all knew that Madeline had her fair share of boyfriends but what we didn't know were the type of boyfriends she had on her leash."

Revealing an image of Madeline and their math's teacher who had recently resigned from Harrington, Mr Addams, Scarlett felt some sort of satisfaction within her. Kissing underneath a palm tree in the Bahamas, Madeline seemed unaware of the snaps of photographs being taken less than 5 metre from her. For someone who's been under the spotlight for so long, one would think she would spot them without blinking her eye.

"Remember Mr Addams?" she asked. "He resigned this September and it's not hard to put the pieces together on why he did so. Madeline's done this on multiple of occasions: Mr Richards, Sir Carlisle, Mr Landon, and the list goes on."

Leaning forward, Scarlett's eyes narrowed. "Why she does it? That's how she's been succeeding, how she's passing those exams with flying colours whilst the rest of us work hard. The girl is nothing but a blonde airhead. Let's not forget that she's a raging alcoholic, drinking too much whilst simultaneously hooking up with guys left, right and centre."

She pulled out a laminated picture from Madeline Vos' file, the camera blurred before converging on the compromising image — a photography that would put the Vos name to shame. Madeline's legs were crossed, but not over her own. One leg outstretched with coke trailing up to the hems of her dangerously short skirt with a guy bent beside it, back to the camera. Another leg was tangled with the boy she was sitting on, her manicured hands cupping his face as she angled his head to kiss him, her body barely covered, her dainty hands clasping onto a champagne glass.

"High school sweetheart, more like high school slut."

"How long is this one going to last?" Elijah chortled.

Madeline scowled. "Shut up."

Celeste smiled, it wasn't her usual evil smile or the smile that threatened to expose you, it was a smile of pure amusement. Besides her, Bentley was avoiding the gaze of Akari and vice versa, Scarlett had no doubt that it was about what occurred over summer whilst Celeste had been at 'summer school' — at least that's what her mother told everyone.

"Celeste Leon. Where did she go last summer? Freshman year, then sopho-more year."

The scene changed just as Scarlett paused; it was brief and unless you were focusing carefully, you wouldn't have seen it, but it was there. Her eyes flickered down nervously, her hands faltered on the evidence in front of her. However, as if something had clicked within her, all signs of hesitance disappeared. In front of her sat a more formal piece of evidence — it looked like some type of documentation.

"She never went to summer school," Scarlett began, holding up an ad-mission form that Celeste's personal details and information. "Our queen, the centre of our god damn school, was admitted to a boarding school in Switzerland. During freshman year, her parents divorced and what we didn't see was our princess going haywire and let's say she caused too many scandals, tarnishing her mother's perfect reputation. So, having to protect that, her mother sent her to Switzerland where they 'helped her get better.'"

Scarlett frowned mockingly, tilting her head to the side as she provided photographic imagery of Celeste at an institute, wearing a disgustingly pale blue uniform that could be mistaken for a nurse outfit. Her lush ebony hair was tied back roughly into a ponytail, her face bare from makeup, revealing dark circles under her eyes, her features dainty and fragile as if was she glass. She sat underneath a tree, concentrating on the book she was reading, oblivious to her surroundings. In another photo, the same location, a lady — a nun — came up to hand, handing her what seemed like pills.

"Let's not forget that she was reinstituted during sophomore year, only it wasn't her parents who sent her. But, her boyfriend," Scarlett laughed, her eyes crinkling, throwing her head back. "Poor Celeste. Two different occasions, I guess that's what they call a relapse. Your daddy is gone and now, not only your mother thinks you're gone crazy, but so does your loving boyfriend, let alone all those publications. I wonder what they're giving you for you to still act as if you're much better than everyone, because let's face it..."

Scarlett's tone darkened as she paused, every word she said held venom, every symbol she emphasised with disgust. It wasn't hard to tell how much she hated the Elites, Celeste mostly. Her eyes narrowed, the corner of her lips curled into a scowl, she scrunched her fist as she spat out her words of odium.

"You're the lowest of the low."

"Fresh meat?" Elijah teased; his eyes burned with mischief when he noticed a group of girls cowering slightly under the gaze of Harrington's elites. "Can't wait to try that out."

Scarlett clenched her jaw and did her best to hold back her disgust, but her hands shook underneath the table with rage, detestation, but also fear. He sat opposite her, ignoring her but as spoke so carelessly about those girls, it felt as if he was targeting her. She wanted to kill him, to choke him, for him to suffer for everything he has done to her, to Florence, and many other innocent girls. But, she couldn't. She had to sit across him quietly, good-naturedly chatter with him and act as if he didn't completely shatter her.

"You're such a perv," Madeline said, wrinkling her nose.

He smirked at her. "You know you love it."

"Go to hell."

"Only if you come with me."

She opened her mouth to retort but Celeste interrupted, coughing loudly to break up the bickering between Madeline and Elijah. Celeste's eyes pinched together when she noticed Madeline about to argue, but the blonde quickly thought against it and glowered. Elijah grinned with triumph, enjoying the look of defeat across Madeline's face.

Scarlett suddenly had the urge to throttle him across the table and, as if she had read Scarlett's thoughts, Akari grabbed her hands, squeezing them softly. Scarlett couldn't hide the look of disbelief, her eyes widening at the Japanese girl who evidently avoided her gaze. It pained Scarlett, a scar that reminded her of what needed to be done.

"Elijah Astor," The girl with crimson hair said, her grey eyes shakily staring at Elijah's file. Her hands shook, a slight tremor, a reminder of what happened and how it was a part of her. "See, Elijah is an illusion, a lie. Everyone thinks he's the friendliest out of all the Elites — sure, he's humorous and charming but it's a lie."

She trembled. She looked like shattered glass, her eyes heavy and tired, the makeup covering how pale she actually looked. Scarlett knew it within her that she no longer was the same person. Her reflection was a misrepresentation of who she actually was. Her feelings were hidden underneath the layers of pain, hate and anger; she forgot how to feel.

Briefly, she thought of her best friend — Candace. What would she think of her? Would she still love her? She wanted to apologise, to admit that the Elites weren't as remarkable as she thought they were, that she should've listened. Maybe none of this would've happened, maybe she wouldn't be looking in the camera as if she was a ghost, a tainted past.

"On many accounts, Elijah has sexually assaulted numerous of girls and have gotten away with it because his daddy is a top-notch lawyer in New York," she began, pausing to gather her thoughts before continuing. "Too many girls had suffered under Elijah's hands, too many girls paid or threatened to stay quiet, too many girls who's been stripped away their right to say 'no'. A young freshman, naïve and innocent, scarred because of Elijah. I was one of those girls."

The tears formed up in her silver eyes, but she quickly blinked them away; she didn't want to cry, she had to stay strong. Pursing her lips to hold back a sob, she wiped the loose tears off her cheeks and plastered a pained smiled.

"This summer, at Celeste's party, a gathering to celebrate the end of a year. It was harmless fun, the whole lot of it; drinking, dancing, talking and laughing. It was supposed to be fun, to be a time to relax and not stress up the future. Maybe one or two hours in, hanging with the Elites you get drunk pretty quickly; let's not forget the drugs. Kaito brought in everything and anything, from marijuana to crack. The table was scattered with different coloured pills and I was lost in the ecstasy of it all.

"That was the norm. It was fun. I was never a drug type of person, I always stayed away from it, but the Elites showed me a whole new world. I was grateful. At first. I don't know when it happened, how it happened or why it happened. I just remember being trapped in the room, screaming at him, begging him to let me go until my throat was sore. He didn't let me go."

She swallowed the cry, looking away from the camera. Her shoulders slugged as if they were holding weight as she nervously twitched her hands on the table, one hand anxiously rubbed her throat as if she was remembering the pain.

"He wasn't drunk, he wasn't high. He knew what he was doing, and he still did it. He broke me. The worse part was that the next morning, laying naked on a bed in one of Celeste's guest room, on the table besides me, was an envelope — my name written in cursive letters. Inside was a cheque of $5,000,000. He acted as if he could compensate me for what he had done. He was threatening me to stay quiet. So, I did. At least, I wanted to."

"What about them?" Akari sniggered, glancing at the couple behind them; freshmen no doubt, hand entwined as they enjoyed each other's company. "They look fun to toy with."

"Akari," Scarlett frowned in disapproval, fully aware on the reason behind Akari's actions.

She ignored her, looking at Celeste with anticipation — the queen pondering over Akari's suggestion before her grin widened, eyes sparking with gleam. She only nodded slightly but that was enough for Akari to jump out of her seat and terrorizing the young couple.

She was a sheep under Celeste's control, mindlessly following the orders of the French beauty whilst tormenting the innocent students. Bentley watched the Japanese girl, his brows furrowed as he leaned forward. Scarlett knew exactly why he showed concern towards her, she was surprised that Celeste hadn't put the pieces together.

Guess she didn't know everything.

Besides her, Zane sighed in annoyance, looking away from the scene. The couple was humiliated under Akari's actions, scared and embarrassed as the cafeteria laughed at them whilst Akari pouted innocently, one hand on the table as she towered over them.

"Cute," she taunted. A smirk plastered across her face, wiggling her brows, Akari enjoyed the look of fear that was on their face — it only fuelled her hunger for power. "Welcome to Harrington."

"Oh, Akari," Scarlett exhaled and held up the filed with Akari's name written on it besides Bentley's. "I wish you defended me instead of choosing them. I came you, Akari. I told you what happened with Elijah and you told me to never speak about to, that he was joking and didn't mean it. I don't understand why you are so loyal to a group who wouldn't think twice in dismissing you. Why do you try so hard to please Celeste? The guilt must be killing you."

Tipping the file upside down, nothing was revealed. Empty. It was all a game, a game that Scarlett knew how to play so well. The Elites taught her well and here she was — about to take them off the throne. It was time for someone else to rule.

"Honey, if Celeste knew your secret, you'd be dead meat. But, let's save the best for last. I want to see Celeste's face when I reveal the truth. I told you to be on my side and now look at what I'm going to have to do. I didn't want to do this to you, but it's sadly come down to this," Shaking her head, she pouted patronisingly before shrugging unbothered. "You can't rule once you lose your financial status and, once your secret comes out, that's exactly how Celeste will be. Then, I'll take the crown that Celeste bares."

Standing up from her seat, Scarlett tucked a strand of loose her behind her ear and reached out towards the camera.

"This isn't the end," she stated; a sadistic look crossed her face as her lips curled into a smile, wide and filled with promises to cause chaos. "We still have Winter Formal."

Video end.

-

What's Akari's secret?

- fariha.

- -

Chapter XIV: Puzzle

You apologise, but why?

Stop saying sorry. It wasn't your fault, Scarlett.

They hurt you, ruined you and tore you apart as if you were a doll. It was their fault alone.

I love you.

Sent by Candace at 6:00 A.M.

***

HARRIS SAT IN front of me, a warm cup of coffee in his hands as he gazed out the window aimlessly, watching the cars drive by. Opposite him, I sat quietly, sipping on tea which warmed my inside during this cold day. It had been approximately 4 days, 6 hours and 23 minutes since I last had contacted someone, since I've found out Zane's secret, since I watched the video.

My phone rang relentlessly, Stryker's name popping up, but never once did I answer it. I avoided him during lunch, lesson and anywhere where he'd usually be. I couldn't bear to face him, to look him in the eyes and pretend that nothing happened. Over the last few days, a realisation had hit me — I had feelings for Zane. That was a problem, a huge problem for me because I couldn't get myself involved with him. I had no doubt that once he found out what I've been doing, he'd never look at me the same way again — he wouldn't want to even be near me.

A part of me pained at the thought of that happening, but it was inevitable.

"So?" he asked, breaking the silence. His eyes flickered over to me; he wanted an answer, he wanted to know, but I knew, behind those layers he had shielded up, he was afraid to hear the truth. "What was in the video?"

Sighing, I placed my cup down, running my hands through my hair. The video. Watching Scarlett as she carefully revealed the hidden secrets of the Elites, but, at the same time, speaking amicably to the Elites during lunch. I hesitated, trying to gather my thoughts, anxiously bouncing my legs underneath the table. I clasped my hands together, leaning forward, his eyes tentatively waiting for my reply.

"There's not much to say," I began. "Scarlett mentioned something about the Winter Formal. Did you record anything that day?"

He frowned. "Why are you avoiding my question?"

"Can you answer my question?"

"Answer mine first."

For the longest minute, we had a stare off, waiting to see who would give in first. His eyes creased together as he adamantly refused to speak so I exhaled, leaning back in the chair as I took a sip of my coffee. The weather was cold today, white sheets of snow had melted away and left in its place the wet, icy ground. January used to be my favourite month, a fresh new year, a fresh new start — so, why did it feel like I was still in the past?

"Do you really want to know, Harris? Are curious or do you just want to feel less guilty?" I asked. He gave no reply. "Because, if you want to know, I'll tell you what I watched, what I heard. But that's only if you really and truly want to watch."

He didn't answer me, steadily holding my eyes and I knew he was conflicted, different types of emotions flickering through the depth of his eyes, but one thing stood out for sure — fear. The fear of the unknown. He was scared, that was all I needed to know his answer.

"Did you guys record during Winter Formal?" I repeated.

Harris shook his head, glancing down. "No. Scarlett told me not to, I would get caught and she didn't want to risk that. The venue we were at was the Harrington Hotel, she mentioned that the hall we had rented out and smaller rooms all had security cameras — I think she was going to use those."

"Will you be able to find the one she was going to use?"

"I'm not sure. So much happened during that night, I have no doubt that most of the footage would've been destroyed before it even hit sunlight. It's how the Elites got away with so much, Bentley held the ropes of the entire building."

"I need that tape, Harris," I pleaded. "I need it. Please, just try."

He looked hesitant, I could almost see the clogs turning in the back of his head before he sighed, nodding. "It's going to take some time. Maybe a few days max."

I grinned before taking his hand, squeezing it comfortingly. Big, brown eyes stared at me, a hint of sadness swam within them and my heart tightened.

"Thank you, Harris."

*

I couldn't stop myself from replying the video over and over again. Hearing her speak, her laughter, the way her eyes creased, how she held back the tears and anger. I wanted to call her, ask her how she's doing, but I knew she wasn't going to answer — she never did. I remembered about the last time we spoke; guilt clouded my judgment and reminded me of what has happened.

That's why I was doing this, so that she'd forgive me and that she'd finally be in peace. Just as I was about to restart the video, my phone rang — Akari's name blinked on the screen. I frowned, confused to why she's calling this late at night before reluctantly picking up.

"Come over right now," she said before hanging up.

I blinked in shock.

It took me a long time to process what just occurred, glancing at my phone in surprise. Once I gathered what just happened, I moved off my bed, dressing up quickly before rushing off to her home. As usual, her home was eerily empty; it made no sense why she'd live in such a large home by herself — especially if her brother is barely around. I knew the place like the back of my hand, entering the home with the key hidden in the plant pot, glancing around to see if Kaito was home.

I frowned, slowly closing the door as I called her name out. I got no reply, instantly my mind ran off to irrational thoughts and fear greeted me. Momentarily, I wondered if I should go home when I heard a quiet sob from upstairs. The rational part of me was telling me to leave, turn away from this right now, but I couldn't help myself as I climbed up those stairs, closing the distance between me and her bedroom. Gingerly, I entered the room where I saw her, face in her hands, her body shaking as she released quiet sobs, curled on the floor besides her bed.

"Akari?" I whispered. Her crying stopped before she looked up, a tear-stained face with flushed cheeks.

"You came," It sounded more like a question than a statement.

"Of course, I'd come," I could almost picture the devil on my shoulder snickering as I moved towards her. "What's wrong?"

"I had an argument with Celeste, I confronted her, and it all went to shit," she cried. "I said things I shouldn't have said and now... Candace, she's threatening to ruin my career."

Settling besides her on the floor, I wrapped my arms around her, wondering if it was a good time to tell her about the photo and videos Celeste had. "I'm sorry."

"It's my fault. I shouldn't have gotten involved in the first place. I messed up because I got too cocky and now, I am paying for my sins," Akari rambled, crying into my chest. "God, I did everything for her. I wanted to impress her, for her to like me. The sacrifices I made for her."

I frowned in confusion, opening my month to ask when she interrupted, a crazed look in her eyes as she glanced up, shaking her head as if she was trying to convince herself about something.

"I gave up everything for her, Candace. Everything. And I understand that it was my fault our relationship has gotten so bad, that I was so stupid and naïve to think that I was worth the same as her, but I lost so much,

Candace. So much. I can still feel the hole in my heart, in my body. And, I did it for her. I lost a part of Bentley for her."

My mind raced with possible theories as she sobbed, in a hysterical state, repeating over and over again about what she lost. But, never once did she clearly say what happened; she was vague and, even though her mental state was anything but normal, Akari never revealed the full truth. It was all pieces, like a puzzle and something was missing to complete the picture. I wanted to speak but she didn't let me.

"Akari?" Snapping my head to the doorway, I saw Bentley staring at the girl in my arms with concern, his expression dramatically different to when he's with his girlfriend, his future — Celeste. "What happened here?"

Akari didn't say anything, stunned, before she collapsed in tears again. Bentley rushed over to her side, not interested with my presence as he took her into his arms, quietly soothing and rocking her. I watched in surprise, stumbling onto my feet — neither Bentley nor Akari glanced my way as I left, too invested in each other. Once I was out the room, I pressed myself against the wall, I held my hand against my mouth to prevent any sounds coming out because, god forbidden, if Bentley heard I was still around — I don't even know what he'd do.

"What's wrong, Kari?" he asked when her sobs settled down to short hiccups. "Who made you cry?"

"I didn't think you'd come," she mumbled. "She doesn't deserve you."

There was no answer at first, I could almost picture him stiffen up; it was clear who she was talking about. Then, a ragged sigh. "It's more complicated than that, Akari, and you know that."

"I wish I didn't. I wish you wasn't with her," she whispered brokenly. "What about us?"

My breath hitched, eyes widening as the puzzle pieces began to fall into place.

"There is no us," he replied icily. "You're hurting yourself by believing there could be."

"You don't love her, Bentley. I know the truth. You chose her, but you don't love her. So, why do I catch you staring at me when you think that I won't notice? Why does your gaze follow me while you're with her? I have so many questions, but I think they can all be answered with just one. Why did you choose her if you want me?" she begged frantically. "Please, please don't go to her. Stay here. With me. I need you. We could've had a future together and she stole that from us. She stole my future."

"Akari, stop this," His words were unheard over her cries. "Don't think for a second that it didn't hurt me to leave you. It was the most painful thing that I've ever had to do. It was so difficult. It took every strength that I had to not turn around and apologise."

There was this cold moment where neither of them spokes; I felt the temperature drop dramatically before I heard a sharp breath of air being taken in.

"So, don't tell yourself that I wanted to. I didn't, not at all. But, leaving you was the only way I could save myself," Bentley whispered, his soft and regretful tone surprising me. I didn't even realise Bentley Harrington was capable of feeling remorseful, it stunned me to no ends.

"You were selfish, Bentley. You leaving me was the worst decision you could've made," she breathed. "Because the second you turned away from me, was the same second I decided to lose the child. Our child."

The world stopped, my heart plummeted and the air thickened as I held back my gasp, my eyes wide like saucers, my back pressed right up against the cold wall.

Akari.

Bentley.

Child.

All the pieces fell in its place and I finally saw the picture, the truth behind everything. I understood it so clearly, everything made so much sense. Scarlett knew this and knew its power. It was like the final straw that held the group together, and once it came out, the group would collapse like marbles.

"You never gave us a chance," Akari murmured. Bentley inhaled sharply before he replied; his tone glacial and emotionless.

"Because there was nothing to give a chance to."

*

Akari was my friend.

That was the only thought constantly rattling in my mind. Although, my intention with her wasn't pure at first, now the mere thought of exposing her curled my insides. She had trusted me, allowing me to enter her world when the others had shut me out, and here I stood alone in the Central Park, watching the glittering stars in the night, lightening up the lone sky, contemplating whether I should expose her or not. I wish it wasn't Bentley. Why did she fall for Bentley?

Tears spiked up in my eyes, my arms wrapping around my body to shelter myself from the glacial air. The park was deserted, yet the streets were busy with life despite the fact that it was twelve in the morning. I was too invested in my thoughts that I didn't release the boy with grey eyes standing across the park. I didn't realise him walking towards me or how he smiled or how he called my name.

I didn't even glance his way, steadily keeping my eyes on the sparkling diamonds. It wasn't until he took my hand, cupping the side of my face when I finally broke out of my spell, my eyes snapping over to his. There was a frown, his eyes mirroring the concerned expression painted across his face.

"What are you doing out here alone?" he asked but he sounded so far away.

Numbly, I replied, "Needed air. Why are you here?"

"I usually stroll through the park whenever my stepmother was home. I needed some space from the house," he answered. "Are you okay?"

No. No, I wasn't okay. I felt like a broken glass, my emotions were everywhere, my thoughts were incoherent, and yet, I knew one thing for sure. I was clearly in love with Zane Stryker. Bright grey eyes, almost silver, studied me barely as he caressed my cold cheek with his thumb, sparking warmth across my body. He tilted his head to the side; a small smile replaced his frown as he closed the distance between us. He was everything I could have, but I knew I couldn't.

"I'm sorry," I whispered.

He chuckled softly. "Why? You've done nothing wrong."

"You must be so cold," I lied.

"Not at all. In fact, I'm very warm but you on the other hand..."

He trailed off as he slipped the jacket off his shoulders and slugged it around mine, his cinnamon scent evaded my senses, his jacket offering me all the warmth I needed in that moment. And I felt like a fraud for taking it.

"How about we grab some hot chocolate?"

Shaking my head, I sighed as I held the coat tighter against my body. "I should get home."

He looked reluctant to let me go, opening his mouth to argue but thought better against it, and instead nodded with a tender smile, which made me feel warm during this cold night. He tucked his blue hands into his pocket, unaffected by the icy wind as it breezed past us.

"I'll see you at school," Zane said.

"Goodnight," I smiled and turned away from him, ignoring the cracks forming within my heart as I walked away.

I didn't get far when I heard him call my name out, my eyes glancing over my shoulder as I halted. His face held so many emotions it was hard to tell what he was feeling but then he encased my hands into his and pulled me closer against him, a bubble of warmth engulfing us, before he gently kissed me.

At first, I was shocked, my eyes wide as I froze but a moment later, I melted into his hold, relaxing the tension on my shoulders, unaware of his jacket dropping onto the ground and how the cold bit against my skin. I melted like ice cream, his arms curling around my waist as if he knew my knees had become weak.

The world had stopped and if it was possible, the cold had disappeared, every fibre of my body set alight as adrenaline rushed through me. My hands moved up to his shaggy hair, tugging them as every reasonable and sane thought left me. The sudden urge to tell him everything, from the beginning to the end, overwhelmed me, alongside the torturous feeling of love.

I felt his lips quirk into a small smile when we kissed, a reminder that what seems so innocent may not be at all. I wanted to be with him. I guess that was why I pulled away from him abruptly with wide shocked eyes.

Because I knew I could never be with him.

My hands removed itself from his chestnut hair, my finger touching his lips as reality came thundering down. He looked at me with confusion, the distance between us might not be large but it sure did feel like we were miles apart. My breathing had become laboured alongside his as we stared at each other, unsure of what of to do or what to say. There was too much that had happened, too much that we were keeping away from each other. That was probably why I walked away; I didn't look back; I didn't say a word — I just walked away.

And the cold greeted me, a reminder that I was alone.

*

I sent the file... or more like files. I thought it would be best to combine them, so you have the full event of that night. You got lucky that I was able to find it quickly — don't ask how. I hope this answers your questions.

— Harris

My finger wavered over the file that blinked on my screen. I wasn't sure if I was ready for this, to know the truth of what happened that night. My heart hammered against my ribs like a caged animal, I could hear my blood rushing and my body suddenly felt numb and heavy. Was this truly what I needed? Would it give me peace? Would it finally give Scarlett peace?

"Don't do it," she whispered, her legs crossed over the other as she settled besides me. "You're not ready. It's too early."

"I need to know the truth," I stated firmly yet I heard the fear shaking in my voice.

"This won't help you," Soft like a feather her voice was, but it also was icy like the winter snow. Out of habit, she tucked a strand of red hair behind her ear, that told me she was anxious and nervous. So was I. "Reconsider—"

She was abruptly cut off as my phone shrilled, Akari's name blinking on the screen. I didn't dare pick up but after two calls, she left a message instead. Peering down at the gadget beside me, I read the message.

Thanks for tonight, C.

I'm sorry I was a mess and that you had to leave so quickly. I'll make it up to you with a spa day and treat you out ;)

Also, don't mention to anyone about Bentley. Can't have Celeste thinking that there's something going on between us.

Love you lots.

— Akari.

Deception.

It was the Elites favourite game to play. I glanced at the girl besides me, who frowned at her former friend's message, before glancing at the file when I made my decision. I exhaled, closing my eyes, hearing the whispers of her last words.

"I did it to myself."

When I opened them, she was gone and all that was left of her was the file blinking on my screen.

This is for you, Scarlett. I'm doing this for you.

Without another thought, I clicked the file and allowed the tape to roll.

Next chapter is the big one.

What do you think is going to happen?

- fariha.

15 | winter formal, junior year

HER RED HAIR was unmissable as she sauntered through the crowd, adoring a smile she scouted the hall to find a particular green-eyed girl in amidst of the swaying drunk bodies as the loud music reverberated around them.

Celeste Leon.

From afar, the 'Queen' of Harrington noticed the girl who threatened to steal her crown; she rolled her eyes as she turned to her best friend, who stood idly besides her, snarling at the sight of Scarlett Lockwood — a snarl that could've been mistaken for smirk by people surrounding them. Madeline whispered something to Celeste which caused her to snicker, an interaction Scarlett spotted as she closed the distance between them, and it caused her entire mood to sour — an expression clear on her face.

"Powder room. 10 minutes," Scarlett ordered, momentarily holding Celeste's eyes, whose looked anything but friendly.

When did Lockwood call the shots? Wasn't Celeste the Queen? Maybe that's why she sneered at the redhaired girl. Scarlett smirked. Then, she turned away, slipping through the crowd whilst greeting everyone and anyone who glanced her. Her eyes steadily focused on the bar — a drink would surely make this evening more enjoyable. At the bar, greeting Scarlett, was the lone Japanese twin, the eldest by 10 minutes, cocking his head to the side as he raised a brow at the sight of her.

"Ah, my beautiful aka," Kaito smirked when she settled besides him, his eyes twinkled. "Looking quite ravishing this evening."

A scoff left her red lips. "Order me a drink, Kaito. Also, where's your sister?"

"Lockwood is calling the shots now," He kissed his teeth in disapproval, yet his amused expression said otherwise. "I heard you want to gather in the powder room. Did Celeste ask for that?"

Of course, Celeste. It's always about Celeste. Why does Celeste decide when they meet? Why is she the only person calling the shots? Scarlett's face darkened as she shook her head.

"No. I did. Now, get me that drink and tell me where your sister has disappeared to. I told her to meet at the front a while ago."

"I'm not her babysitter."

Rolling her eyes, she had no doubt the twins had gotten in yet another argument. She wondered for a second if Akari had finally found out about Kaito's true business, maybe that was why they were arguing. But, there was a huge chance it could be about their father — Kaito has never had a good relationship with their father. Once a drink sat in front of her, she wasted no time as she swallowed it all, ignoring the look of amusement from Kaito.

The alcohol sparked a buzz within her, adrenaline rushing through her body. It was a good feeling, she loved it, she relished in it. Handing the glass back to the bartender, she set off on her journey, pushing through sweaty bodies in search of Akari — instead she found Elijah Astor.

"Kaito's listening to you," The corner of Elijah's lips lifted up in a sadistic smile, his eyes clearly showing he was too far gone. "That's the first. We're taking orders from you now?"

Scarlett's nose crinkled in disgust. Briefly, she wished Candace was her; she would protect her from him. He clasped her head as he lifted it up to his lips where his alcohol stained lips pressed against her porcelain skin. Hazel eyes studied her features with interest when she snatched her hand back.

"My queen," he mocked. "What would you like me to do?"

"I'd like you to find me Akari."

She knew he was making her uncomfortable on purpose, like a prey to a predator; Elijah liked to play with his toys, no matter how broken they were, he'd just tear them further apart until there was nothing left of them. A game. It was all a game. However, now she knew how to play it perfectly. This time she was going to win.

"Of course."

Tightening her jaw, she sent him a hard look before sauntering away, grabbing a glass from the waiter's tray and sipping on it quickly, discarding it when another walked past, and then taking one more. The alcohol gave her the confidence that Celeste battered down; it made her feel invincible, powerful and she savoured it, finishing her sixth glass tonight.

She was not usually this drunk but tonight would be a momentous occasion, she needed all the confidence and strength she could possible muster up, and the anxiety bubbling within her wasn't helping at all. Drinking around the Elites was a dangerous move, albeit, tonight, Scarlett couldn't care less. Outside Harrington hotel, puffs of smoke greeting her, was the heir himself and his best friend as they inhaled the joint whilst discreetly conversating.

"Boys," she purred, snatching the joint out of Zane's hand.

His eyes narrowed at her with annoyance whilst Bentley looked entertained, his eyes crinkled with amusement. That wasn't good. Bentley only found joy in dark and twisted things, that should've been a warning to Scarlett. She naively ignored it.

"Scar," Bentley said. "You look beautiful tonight."

Doing a little twirl, she grinned. "You think? Do I look better than Celeste?"

It was a dangerous line that she was crossing, but she loved it. The thrill of seeing the power couple argue over her. It would oh–so entertaining that she couldn't help herself but to tease. To flirt. His eyes darkened, not with lust but delight.

"Careful, Lockwood."

Her smiled broadened as she sent him a wink before turning to Zane, who was carefully watching her.

"Why are you here?" Zane asked coolly, drawing in the joint, sounding disinterested. His tone immediately put Scarlett off, a pout replacing her grin as she wacked his arm, earning herself a glare.

"I'm offended. I thought we were friends," she whined, a sound that clearly put Zane off as he sighed, tossing the cigarette to the floor.

"Don't speak like that, Scar. Doesn't suit you," he retorted insultingly, before slipping back into the venue. Cocking her head to the side, she watched him in confusion — he wasn't usually this rude with her.

"Where is my beau?" Bentley asked, steering Scarlett attention away from Stryker and onto himself, a hand in his pocket as he coldly stared her down.

"Somewhere inside. I think I saw her flirting with some guy," she lied, running her hand through her hair. The alcohol was really taking her affect and she feared that it would disappear before the main event. Now, she couldn't let that happen. But, at the same time, she couldn't stop herself as she leaned closer to Bentley, curling her lips into a suggestive smile. "You could do so much better, Bent. If anything, I've always seen you with Akari."

Her words had an impact on him; his eyes iced, his jaw clenched as his back stiffened, a glare promising to dig a grave for the redhead. She was amused. She couldn't help it. Anticipation alongside with alcohol just made this game all more exciting, and, for the first time since she'd become an Elite, she had the upper hand. She knew something that they didn't. That even Kaito didn't know. And that was exhilarating.

"I think you've had one to many drinks, Lockwood," he answered in a glacial tone. "Don't make such a suggestion again."

Scarlett knew better than to push Bentley too far and reigned in, quickly laughing and masking a look of innocence, but she was pretty sure her flushed cheeks did that for her.

"I'm joking, Harrington. So uptight," she snorted. "That's not why I came out here anyways. I wanted to tell you that we are meeting in the powder room. All of us. I expect to see you there."

Something must've amused Bentley when a sadistic smirk graced his face as he disregarded the cigarette onto the floor. Even though, the night was cold, standing in front of Bentley Harrington was much colder. It was dangerous. And Scarlett loved dangerous.

"Celeste?"

Although he spoke of one word, Scarlett knew what he was asking — it was all anyone was asking this evening. Did Celeste summon us? It infuriated her to no ends. Why did no one understand that she had power to summon the group? It wasn't fair that Celeste had so much control. Scarlett had done her best to ensure she could overthrow Celeste, even though she didn't want to in the first place.

All Scarlett wanted was to be popular, the centre of attention, to ensure that Harrington was ruled in safe hands, and she couldn't be Celeste's best friend — Madeline Vos already took that spot. Celeste went out of her way to ensure that Scarlett would always be an outsider; it didn't matter whether she was invited to all these gatherings or sat on the centre table, Celeste isolated her. That was annoying.

Scarlett knew that she was never going to stop and that she will never be able to repair the balance in Harrington Preparatory unless Celeste was ripped away her right to have such a control. She worked small; she was clever. She started from Akari, weeding her way into her innocent heart, planting lies and deception, manipulating her to think that Celeste had something huge against her — that's probably how their friendship began to crack.

Akari's paranoia did the rest of the job. Then she got into Zane, the person who invited her to the Elites, a friend. Expect, she didn't want to be friends with him; she wanted more. Nevertheless, they were friends, close friends therefore she ensured that whenever Celeste did something to hurt her, she'd run to Zane, plaster on her best victimised look with tears streaming down her face. Zane was like putty in her hands. Next, you had Kaito and Elijah.

They were much more difficult like titanium, they were unable to crack however, Scarlett wasn't going to give up and gathered that if she couldn't break them, she'd at least chip them - she knew they'd do the rest of the job themselves. The last two in the Elites were too loyal, to a certain extent, to Celeste therefore Scarlett didn't waste time on them. She knew that the secret between Akari and Bentley would be enough to shatter them. From there, she'd take the throne.

Don't get justice and revenge mixed up, Candace had once mentioned but that before she called Scarlett a manipulative bitch who was obsessed with the entire system. Scarlett was not obsessed, she wanted to serve justice for everyone the Elites had hurt. Scarlett knew that Candace thought her dream was a joke, that the entire Harrington hierarchy was laughable, but Scarlett knew otherwise.

One could almost call it a work of art and to maintain the authenticity of such a masterpiece, one must ensure that any frauds must be removed. The frauds being the Elites. Dropping a status was social humiliation and something hummed in satisfaction within Scarlett whenever she thought about that.

"No," She walked away. "It was me."

She didn't want to see the look on Bentley's face, and glided back into the venue, grabbing two glasses from a passing waiter, drinking it down too quickly that it made her feel sick. She ignored that. The alcohol was making her lightheaded, the champagne along with the vodka that she had at the bar had taken its toll, but she stupidly ignored it, mistaking it for confidence as she sauntered towards the powder room where she was stopped by Harris, someone she once sat with when she was in the third clique —the person that was helping her take down the Elites. He couldn't stomach the idea of going against the Elites, it infuriated her that he backed out when she needed him the most.

"Scarlett, I need to tell you something," Harris demanded.

She scowled. "Can't it wait? I'm busy."

Moving past him, his hands reached out and grabbed her wrist, yanking her to him. The look of desperation was clear on his face, he was so conflicted that it left Scarlett feeling unsettled. Her mouth opened to protest but someone else spoke first as they jerked her away from Harris.

"Leave her alone, freak," Kaito snarled, the disgust on his face would make one think Harris was some sort of infection.

"Scar—"

"I said, piss off."

Dragging Scarlett away from Harris, all she could think was the look on his face. He looked guilty, afraid, ashamed, and she wasn't sure way. It was only then she realised she wasn't feeling confident, it was her anxiety skyrocketing.

From the corner of her eyes, she was a flash of black hair and wished she didn't look up because when she did, her eyes locked directly with Celeste's. The cat—eyed girl glowered as she made a beeline towards Scarlett, who suddenly realised that Kaito was no longer besides her.

"This is a bloody joke," Celeste sneered but she looked like a kitten.

It was amusing to Scarlett. Without Madeline ranking her side — no doubt making out with her teacher — or Akari following her tail, Celeste looked defenceless, worthless. Nothing. Scarlett smirked. At the same time, her shields guarded up, an amour to protect her self—esteem from Celeste's piercing words like daggers.

"Stop throwing yourself at my boyfriend, Lockwood. You're reek of desperation. It's not a pretty look for you."

"You'd know what desperation looks like, wouldn't you, Celeste?" Scarlett bit back.

Celeste's cheeks flushed as her eyes spiked into threatening glares. She towered over the redhead with a smile that held no signs of friendliness; it was cold and calculating, dark and menacing. Her voice dropped down a few notches when she whispered words of malicious intent.

"You're nothing compared to me, Lockwood. A slut and traitor. I know what you've done."

Scarlett stiffened when Celeste leaned back with a triumphant smirk, her lips coated in blood red, similar to Scarlett. Although, dressed in different gowns, that evening the pair look like the same people. Black hair bounced as Celeste turned away from the redhead, throwing her words back to her before she disappeared into the crowd.

"Powder room. 10 minutes."

Scarlett was raging in anger. She needed to find Kaito desperately; Kaito had the drugs that would numb the feeling. Once up a time, a few words from Candace was all Scarlett needed to relieve herself from the anger and anxiety, but now, drugs did a better job. Scarlett wondered what Candace was up to, she was probably sleeping soundly whilst her best friend was taking down the villains of this story.

It didn't take long to find the silver-haired boy in the mist of people, mingling with three girls at the counter. All it was one look and Kaito knew what the girl wanted; his smile altering into a smirk as his hand rustling in his pocket in search for something — a small clear packet — and slipping it into her clasp. She shoved herself through the crowd, hiding the packet in her purse, and found Akari perched up close next Bentley, swallowing when she saw the pair lean close, whispering quietly to each other. Akari was a friend, she would support her, she knew she would.

"Akari!" Scarlett yelled and the Japanese girl jumped, eyes wide as her head shot to Scarlett's direction.

Relief swarmed her eyes as she slipped off the chair and elegantly moved towards Scarlett with a bright grin. Scarlett swayed, cursing herself for drinking too much but don't care as she drank more whenever the opportunity came by.

"Where have you been all evening?" Akari asked, her breathing was ragged, and Scarlett had no doubt that she had been making out with Bentley moments before. She was being brave tonight.

"Powder room, Akari. We need to all gather there. Come on," Scarlett slurred as she grabbed Akari's hand, leading her to the destinations despite her protest. "Come on, Kari. Everyone is waiting for us."

"Is Celeste going to be there?" she asked timidly.

"Of course," Scarlett sent her a tipsy grin. "She's the main character."

Akari was confused, Scarlett knew that, but it didn't matter because once the truth was revealed everything was going to be alright. It was all falling into itself place. A game of chess wouldn't work without the queens, and Scarlett was about to make her final move. After climbing the polished, marble stairs, they entered the lavish room.

Like she had hoped, the powder room was empty when they entered; gold themed with spotlights above them — she expected nothing less from the Harrington's. She released Akari and stumbled over to the illuminating mirrors, admiring her reflection despite the fact that she looked a bit of a mess with her mascara smeared and her hair untidy.

As long as her lips stayed red, Scarlett looked beautiful.

"What is going on?" Elijah muttered as they began pouring into the room one by one until all eight members of the Elites were secluded in one location.

"Ask her," Celeste answered dryly.

"What's going on, Scar?" Zane questioned, his eyes creasing in confusion.

Scarlett felt giddy, her phone in her purse burned with evidence, as she grinned up at them. She looked like a right state, her cheeks were flushed from the anxiety and alcohol, her makeup was a wreck, yet she paid no attention to these small details — details that easily became her weakness.

She was too invested in the attention they were feeding her; she basked in it. It set her body alight and a rush shivered through her body. She never usually had their attention, not like this anyways, and she love every second of it. She wanted more, she needed more. That's why she didn't realise the girl with green eyes masterfully planning her dismissal.

"I have big news," she began opening her purse but before she could continue, Celeste interrupted with a broad expression, masking the devious glitter in her eyes.

"If it's drugs, Candace, I'm not in the mood. I saw Kaito handing them to you," she huffed. "Honestly, this is such a waste of my time."

"Not surprised, she looks like she's had one too many," Madeline snickered.

Elijah rolled his eyes. "This is so stupid."

"No, wait!" Scarlett protested, humiliation causing her cheeks to burn as she desperately fought for their attention. For a brief moment, she had it again until she stupidly blurted out, "I never had friends like you guys."

What about Candace? Her subconscious yelled at her. What about your best friend? How can you forget about her?

Celeste looked at her in disappointment, belittling her as she said patronisingly, "I know you've never had friends before us, sweetie. How cute."

Scarlett hated her. The condescending tone that she used. She was degrading her, mocking her, humiliating her. Candace wouldn't have done that. Candace loved her, she adored her. Why did she leave Candace? She wanted Candace.

"Guys, I just want to have fun," she whined.

Madeline snorted. "You're wasted."

"No, I'm not. Come on, the night is still young and there's still show much to show," she grinned suggestively, naively taking out the drugs instead of her phone. Stupid, stupid girl.

Elijah groaned, "Drugs? You called everyone to do drugs? This is stupid."

"Scarlett, maybe that isn't a good idea," Akari, being the voice of reason, said.

"You look like you're on crack anyways," Madeline taunted.

Scarlett frowned. This wasn't what was meant to happen. Usually they'd all agree and would happily comply. Why weren't thing going as planned? Why did she take the drugs out and not the phone? She had to take the phone out. Her heart hammered in her chest and she wanted to burst into tears.

She needed Candace.

Where was Candace?

Bentley tilted his head to the side, unimpressed, and tucked his hands into his pocket. Yet, if you looked closely enough, you'd see how the way his lips twisted into a small smirk — a smirk that said everything that Scarlett needed to know. He knew everything.

She wasn't going to win.

"Enough," he ordered. "If that's all, Lockwood, I'll be leaving."

Scarlett opened her mouth to argue but the Harrington heir had already left the room. Soon after, Kaito and Elijah followed; Zane moved a fraction of a minute after sending her a look of concern — a look that made her feel ill. Scarlett pouted, desperately trying to pick up the pieces — her plan was failing too quickly. But it fell and it was all because of Celeste. Her black hair cascaded past her shoulders as she leaned towards Scarlett with a nasty look on her face.

"I told you I knew what you have done," Celeste whispered. "You made a mistake to trust someone at Harrington."

Scarlett's eyes widened as she registered her words, the pieces clicking together when she remembered the guilty expression painted on Harris's face. He sold her out. Why? Why would he do that?

Celeste teased her, pursing her lips into a shadow of a leer, "You were already high a couple hours ago. I don't think it's a good idea to take some more, you should take my advice if you had any sense."

Burning in utter humiliation, Scarlett glared at Akari, who ratted her out. Akari glanced away in shame, her ivory cheeks colouring red like Scarlett's lips. Scarlett panicked. She was so close; she was nearly there and now it had all been ripped away from her.

"Keep an eye on her," Celeste ordered Akari. "Can't have her tainting the group reputation by looking like a train wreck."

Madeline laughed, fuelling her best friend's ego, as the pair drifted out of the powder room, leaving a deathly silence between Scarlett and Akari. Scarlett felt pathetic and hurt. She hated Celeste Leon, she hated her so much that it was consuming her. She wanted to feel numb, the drugs would make her feel numb. In a state of delusion, Scarlett stumbled over to the sinks, placing the packet of small pills on the vanity as she stared at her reflection.

"Are you going to join me, Akari?" Scarlett questioned in a dead tone.

She knew Akari would be on her side, she was her friend, her only friend at Harrington; she wouldn't let Scarlett be alone. But, that was before Akari hesitantly looked at the state Scarlett was in and slowly shook her head, surprising the girl with red hair. Of course, she would say no; the disapproval from their queen had put her off.

"I'm going to pass. It's too early."

Scarlett's face morphed into something that was in the middle of revulsion and resentment. "Are you serious? You're letting me do this alone?"

"Just don't do it, Scar," Akari pleaded. "Come on, let's grab a drink."

Reaching out for her, Scarlett shrugged her off, shaking her head. "No, thanks. I'll join you in a bit."

"Are you sure?"

"Yes."

Akari looked reluctant, squinting at Scarlett then the drugs, before deciding to leave. The silence cloaked Scarlett, a reminded of how embarrassed she was feeling. She must've looked like a wreck, like an alcoholic. Something Candace once mentioned to her. She didn't believe it back then, but now glancing at her reflection — she didn't know who the girl into the mirror was. All she knew was that she wanted to numb the pain, she had to forget everything. Candace would be so disappointed in her, but Scarlett was far from caring.

She never was a good friend anyways.

Placing the pretty pink pill in her mouth, swallowing it down with tap water, she felt exhilarated as it began to take its effect. She could almost feel every ounce of humiliation and anger disperse into the thin air as she daintily retouched her makeup, painting her lips her favourite colour, the colour of revenge — red. When she was satisfied, the buzz seemed to just get better every second after, she felt like she was powerful, a sickly smirk played on her lips as she admired her reflection.

She'll do everything in her power to destroy Celeste.

With one last promise, she stumbled out the powder room, grappling to find her balance as she giggled witlessly to herself. She was invincible; she could feel it in her bone. Then, she couldn't. One second, she was feeling like she was on top of the world, the next second, she felt as if she was drowning. Hot then cold, her hands felt sweaty and sticky.

She clutched onto the gold banister, trembling as she struggled to see properly; she was so dizzy. Her breathing became laboured, her chest was tight like her lungs had become restrained, her heart was banging against her rib cage like it was screaming, and her stomach cried in pain.

Before she knew it, her weak, frail fingers slipped away from the banister, as she plummeted down the marble staircase. Her bloody, bruised body was on the floor convulsing as foam trickled out her mouth, memories of her and her best friend flickered through her mind.

Candace.

At eleven o'clock, two girls slipped away from the party to pamper themselves. The girl with the green eyes covered her mouth in terror when she took in the situation, whilst the blonde steered her out the hallway not even a second later, blue eyes glancing back in dread. They couldn't be caught here, not when they had their entire future on the line. Celeste Leon and Madeline Vos couldn't risk it. Instead they left, praying that someone else would find her.

At eleven forty, two girls stumbled into the corridor, giggly and intoxicated from the alcohol. The sight of the girl with red hair sprawled across the floor, shaking underneath the diamond chandelier with bile and foam coating the ground, had broken them out their excitement. They immediately called an ambulance.

At twelve, Mrs Lockwood arrived at the hospital in tears, clutching onto her husband's arms as they demanding to see their daughter — their daughter who was now getting her stomach pumped. They didn't understand why this happened; it didn't make sense. The doctors claimed she was in a critical state.

At one twenty-seven, there was a faint heartbeat. Mrs Lockwood desperately kept ringing Candace, who was 3,400 miles away, sleeping soundly, unaware in the situation, unaware of the fifty miscalls she was getting. However, a minute later, it flat lined.

At one forty-six, they tried to revive her through CPR and cardiopulmonary resuscitation.

— But, at two o'clock, Scarlett Lockwood was pronounced dead.

-

Did you expect it?

- fariha.

16 | aftermath

C hapter XVI: Aftermath

I guess some people don't learn their lesson. She knows everything, Celeste. And, he helped her. How foolish of him. I guess we need to teach him a lesson.

Where is his sister right now?

Sent by Madeline at 3:15 A.M.

***

THERE WAS SOMETHING about Scarlett's death that didn't settle with me. Something that made me feel restless and uneasy. It wasn't until I stepped on the same ground as Harrington Preparatory when I knew exactly what it was. Scarlett wasn't dead. She just couldn't come home; I didn't know when she'd come home, but I did know she was in that position because of the Elites. It was never her fault.

They pushed her and pushed her until she saw that going into dangerous boundaries headfirst was the only way she'd survive. For months on end, I wished she stayed in England with me — she would've been safe with me. But, she chose the glitz and glam over her safety, over me. I still love her, I always will. I guess that's why I enrolled myself to Harrington because a large part of me wouldn't rest until I completed what she started. Maybe only then would she come back home.

During the early months after Scarlett's 'death', my mother would ship me off to all different types of doctors and therapists, spending a vast amount of money and time in convincing me that my best friend was dead, but I knew otherwise. They were all liars, they just wanted me to be in pain. That was also probably the Elites doing. They needed to make everyone in Scarlett's life suffer. I wasn't going to let them.

If Scarlett was dead, how come she was still messaging me? Nevertheless, although I couldn't visit Scarlett, her messages were enough for me to know she was okay. I didn't stop watching the recording, I kept replaying it, trying to understand everything that happened during the Winter Formal in Junior Year. Granted, I didn't actually see the interactions within the powder room.

I did see Scarlett drunk smile on her face, which showed she was giddy and excited, as she sauntered through the crowd of people, gathering the Elites. The footage was all over the place, different scenes and locations but watching her wild auburn hair and the bright grin on her red lips, had my stomach churning and my throat constricting.

All eight members of the Elites walked through the arched passageway, leading to a hallway — the only location that didn't have cameras. They'd entered in flocks at different times. Scarlett and Akari, followed by Celeste and Madeline. Then, all four boys — Zane, Elijah, Kaito and Bentley. About half an hour later, they all left in the opposite order as they'd come.

However, only one person never left that place. Scarlett. In fact, she didn't leave the room at all.

Around fifteen minutes later, the Queen of Harrington and her blonde associate re-entered but, in less than thirty seconds, they'd left. Celeste had tears streaking down her face, her lips pursed together, whilst Madeline consoled her, arms wrapped around her best friend as she quietly, and secretively, led her out the venue. I didn't know what happened in there, nor will I ever know, but what happened was their fault — it was all their doing. Maybe if they weren't so wicked, people wouldn't be telling me that Scarlett was dead.

I couldn't bear to watch the entire footage, but I'd seen enough. I saw her challenging Celeste's position. I saw her teasing Bentley. I saw her take the drugs from Kaito despite the fact that she'd been drinking recklessly all night. I saw the red and blue lights reflecting off the mirrored panels across the wall of the Harrington Hotel as the paramedics rushed to the foyer where Scarlett laid unconscious at the bottom of those marble stairs. I had seen it all. And I hated it. I hated them.

There was a tremor in my hands as I pushed the laptop away from me after watching it again for the nth time. It had been days since I left my room, since I stepped foot into Harrington. For a second, I wondered if the Elites cared about my disappearance. My mother wasn't home enough to notice my absence in school, a message to the school via her email was enough for me to not get caught. I pushed open the curtains, squinting as the light blinded me before peeking at my reflection in the mirror.

I was skinny, unhealthy, a wreck. My face was hollow, my body was worn out, dark circles underneath my eyes wouldn't be able to be hidden even with makeup, my face bare from the façade I was used to playing. Then, for a minuscule of a second, I wondered if Scarlett was actually dead. My heart cried out in agony and I banished the doubt from my mind. I move around slowly, cleaning up my surroundings before heading downstairs to brew myself up a coffee when the doorbell rang.

I froze.

The bell rang again.

Slowly, I moved to the door, my breath caught in my throat. Shakily, I reached out for the handle, whether it was from fear or anxiousness – I couldn't tell. Opening the door, my eyes widened when I saw Zane leaning against the wall, dressed in a neat black shirt and jeans. Grey eyes, eyes that reminded me of my best friend, glanced up.

"Zane?" His name was a whisper on my tongue.

"Candace," he said, moving closer. "Can I come in?"

I searched his face, trying to see what the truth was behind his visit, but I saw nothing. He was concerned; his brows creased, a crinkle on his forehead as he examined me. Nodding sluggishly, he slipped into my house, eyes flickering around. The tension between us was rigidity, uncomfortable and strained. The boy I kissed a few days ago sat silently in my living room, whilst I sat opposite him.

"Why are you here?" I spoke first, breaking the quiet.

"Why haven't you been in? It's been nearly a week," he countered back.

"It's been a difficult week. I'm going through some stuff. I wanted to be alone."

"What's wrong? Let me see if I can do anything to help you feel better," Sincerity lanced in his voice only contributed to the crack in my heart.

"You can't help me, Zane."

Silence.

"Why did you run away when I kissed you?"

My breath hitched when he stared at me, demanding an answer to a question I couldn't answer. I shrugged. His face fell, shoulders tightening as the answer I had given wasn't the one he wanted.

"Would you like a drink?"

I had to get away, I had to be as far from him as possible. I needed to leave. Zane moved his head, so I took that as a yes, shuffling into the kitchen. I moved robotically, mindlessly making coffee for the both of us when I heard a phone vibrate. Freezing, I fleetingly thought it was mine before I concluded that it was most likely his –— I wouldn't know what I'd do if he got my phone.

My heart pounded in my chest, the devil on my shoulder laughed at the situation I was in, my breathing was laboured as I lagged my actions, unwilling wanting to spend time with him. But alas, I couldn't leave my guest — my mother would scold me for being a terrible hostess.

"I wasn't sure if you wanted coffee or—" I halted, my eyes widening when I saw him clutching my phone before, slowly, looking at me with pure horror across his face. Everything had smashed right in front of me, the mugs shattering across the ground as my weak hands trembled in fear, coffee spilling across the oak floorboards. "Zane, it's not what it looks like—"

"What the hell is this?" He interrupted, pure fury across his face as he showed me the message blinking on my screen underneath the notification that had exposed me.

I love you too, Candace. Take the Elites down.

— Scarlett

I swallowed roughly, shaking my head slowly as I walked towards him, but he just kept stepping back, keeping a distance between us — like he didn't even want to be near me. My heart clenched and my mind was running with a thousand of excuses but when I opened my mouth, nothing came out.

"Why— No. How are you talking to Scarlett when she's..." he trailed off his sentence, afraid to say the word everyone has been thinking of.

"She's not dead," I gritted out, my face tightening.

"Candace, how are you talking to her when she's dead?"

"She's not dead, Zane!" I yelled in frustration, his facial expression hardening as concerned glistened in his eyes. Or was it guilt? "Stop saying she's dead. She's just abroad right now, she's going to come home soon."

"Candace—"

"Shut up. Stop speaking. Please, stop speaking," My voice turned into a timid whisper as I finished that sentence, stumbling back to find some type of support.

"Scarlett's gone, Candace. She's gone."

I always wondered what it meant when people said their life flashed before their eyes. But, in that moment, mine did. From my first memory of Scarlett to one of my last. Our argument. The night before she returned to New York.

"What is wrong with you, Scarlett!" I screamed, slamming the door to her hotel room. "You didn't need to be so disrespectful to those waiters. I don't understand why you're acting like that!"

She growled, throwing her bag onto her bed. "Oh, shut up, Candace. They shouldn't have messed up my order. It's their job to get it right, it's not my fault that they're incompetent at doing a simple task."

"Are you kidding me? That doesn't give you the right to act like a..." I trailed off, fuming in anger as I fisted my hands, clenching my jaw.

Her hair flipped over her shoulder as she spun around, glaring at me. "Like what?"

Defiantly, she held my gaze. My rage began to settle, but when I saw her brow raise, a small smirk on her face as she closed the distance between us, taunting me when she repeated her question, I couldn't help but burst in anger.

"Like a bitch!"

She doubled over as if my words were like a punch, her face cringing in pain, whilst I heaved heavily. The silence between us was always comfortable and peaceful, words we spoke were never hateful or mean, but that all changed. It changed the second she stepped on that plane 2 years ago. I pursed my lips, pushing past her as I opened the door to the balcony, needing air — I couldn't breathe.

It always physically killed me whenever we got in arguments, that's why we tend not to. I'd give in because I loved her, I loved her so much; I wanted her to be happy. London was beautiful at night, the stars glittering above the skyline, a full moon shining besides the galactic diamonds; I never understood why she loved New York. I felt her presence beside me, cold and distant. It made me feel unsettled, lost, and confused.

"What's happened to us?" I asked.

There was a pause, then quietly, "I don't know. I didn't realise there was something wrong."

"You don't know? You haven't noticed how far we've grown apart? I get that we are on two different continents, but I've never felt so far away from you," I glowered at my best friend. The person I once knew like the back of my hand glared back.

"People can grow apart, you know."

"Obviously," I said, laughing in disbelief. "And obviously you don't care. You're leaving me for new people. Or should I say, more popular people?"

My betrayer gasped and gritted her teeth.

"It's not my fault you're still a loser. Maybe if you grew up a little, you'd be cool and popular. You barely want to go to parties and clubs, so bloody focused on school and the future. Maybe you should let loose and I'll want to be around you."

"I never said I want you to be around me," I replied, measuring my tone carefully whilst steely holding her icy gaze. "You know, I think this is actually for the best. You never did anything for me anyway. Return to New York. Just don't come crawling back to me when your 'new besties' ditch you."

I clutched my chest, leaning against the wall as the horror of the truth came alight, my grief burning within me along with the guilt. For a year, I deluded myself in believing she was alive, that she was going to come back to me one day, but she wasn't — she never will.

Dead.

She was dead.

She was truly gone.

"I loved her," I whispered, hiccupping. "And she's dead."

Zane didn't say anything, his gaze fell on the phone, clenched in his hand. what could he say? He couldn't defend himself, or the Elites? She was dead because of them. Anger bubbled within me as I scoffed, clenching my jaw as I tried to calm down. I closed my eyes, holding the tears that threatened to fall. I wouldn't show him my tears, he didn't deserve my tears. When I opened them, brown eyes staring at me, indifferently looking at me as if I was nothing, as if I was no one.

"I'm sorry, Candace," he said. "I'm sorry, she's..."

There were so many words you could use to describe what Scarlett was: lifeless, deceased, gone. But no one would say it, no one wanted to admit it because once it was spoken then it was out there; the cold, harsh reality.

"Dead. Just say it, Zane," Pursuing my lips, I whispered. "She's dead. And you guys killed her."

*

They know, Candace. They know everything.

— Harris

I had expected that they'd find out. The truth eventually would come to light. Even if Scarlett was dead, that didn't mean I was going to not destroy the Elites. It only gave me more burning passion to. Stepping onto the same land as Harrington Preparatory, I prepared myself to hear insults and lies, to be threatened and violated, but as I walked up the stairs, I didn't encounter anything.

Leaning against the metal stair frame was Kaito and Elijah, drawing in the cigarettes in their hand whilst quietly talking to each other. Elijah saw me first, cocking his head to the side with narrowed eyes, soon Kaito followed after, yet a teasing smirk played on his lips. Gulping inaudibly, I clutched tightly onto my Chanel bag — a gift from Scarlett — licking my red lips as I walked past them. My steps were slow and hesitant, careful and considerate.

I caught Madeline's eyes as she leaned against the locker beside Celeste; the blonde leaned close to her best friend, whispering something. Celeste didn't look my way. Then there was Zane. Strolling down the corridor, hands tucked in his pocket, he walked past me, acting as if I didn't exist.

Bentley watched me from afar, a phone pressed against his ear, but his mahogany eyes stared in my direction — dark and daring. I didn't want to give them the upper hand, let them believe that isolating me would make me less powerful. They made a mistake to let me in the group in the first place.

I needed to find Akari.

My brain worked in a quick motion, surveying the area as I searched for the Japanese girl. I couldn't find her, I needed to find her. I only had Akari left. Then, as if by fate, I saw her sitting in the cafeteria, not in her regular seat, but around the table on the mezzanine — the seat Scarlett once had. She was alone, staring at the centre table, the table that housed the seven members of the Elites plus the ill-fated pawn.

"Akari?" She didn't glance away, her eyes watered. "I need you—"

"Was it a lie?" she asked hesitantly. "Our friendship. Was it a lie?"

"Please, let me explain."

"Don't," she reacted tersely. "You'll make it worse. I have no doubt that you have all you need to ruin us like she would want you too. I can't believe you're the best friend that she adored so much. She kept telling us you're this beautiful blonde from England, smart and quiet, the opposite to her. I should've seen it sooner."

My heart clenched as I shuffled into the seat opposite Akari.

"I shouldn't have stopped Elijah from doing that background check on you," she scoffed.

"Akari, please listen to me," I began, levelling my voice. "You don't belong with them; you aren't like them. You're so much more. Our friendship, Akari. I need you; I need you by my side. They've all done terrible things and I can't let them get away with it. Scarlett died because of them."

"Scarlett died because of me," she argued sharply, knocking the air out my lungs. "I should've dragged her out that room, instead I let her do the drugs even when I knew she had already done some, I left her alone when I should've stayed. I left her."

Akari's hazel eyes moved up, settling on me.

"She didn't deserve it, Candace. Her death changed us. Celeste was quiet, I think the guilt of leaving Scar had left a print on her. For a long time, she wasn't herself until one day she snapped out of it. Madeline was much more overprotective over her, anything that could bring Celeste harm, she dealt with it.

"Bentley, well there's not much to say. He took advantage of Celeste's fragile state, he messed her up even more. Elijah shut out everyone, he became silent. Kaito became reckless — you don't think I know about his business? He needed an outlet, he hated feeling guilty. Zane took it much worse than everyone else — I think he blamed himself."

"They're not good people, Akari. You're telling me this, but it won't change anything," I stated.

She shrugged, standing up. "It probably won't but you need to hear it. They... No... We aren't good people, Candace. I'm one of them, I'll always be one of them."

"You're my friend, Kari. They will never accept you in their group. Celeste despises you, Akari. I'm not going to allow Celeste to ruin your future; Madeline told her that she has videos and pictures that could tarnish your reputation."

Her smile was small, fragile and sad. She didn't look like Akari Takahashi in that won't. She just looked like a girl who's been grieving for a long time.

"If you were my friend, Candace, you should've told me that a long time ago."

Like bullets, her words penetrated my heart, my stomach clamping in grief. She sighed heavily, slouching in exhaustion. And, despite everything that has happened, in the end, there was only one Queen.

"Celeste wants to see you."

-

Theories on the ending?

- fariha.

17 | reign

C hapter XVII: Reign

Dear Ms Lowell,

I regret to inform you that your daughter, Candace, has been slipping in her academic grades and attendance. Since her last formal exam during the beginning of the year, Candace has dropped dramatically in grades.

As an intelligent student, I wish to not dismiss her from Harrington, but her attendance and grades must improve. I am also concerned that she has been focusing primarily on her social status rather than her education.

I think it's best to set up a meeting to consider other options as I fear that if behaviour continues, she will be letting down her future severely. If possible, please email me back as soon as possible.

Best Regards,Mrs AshtonPrincipalHarrington Preparatory

***

TO CELESTE, I was an ant. Tiny, fragile, breakable. She had the world in the palm of her hands. At least, that was what everyone assumed. It was actually Bentley that pulled the strings, Celeste was the puppet to his mastermind game. He manipulated, lied and deceived everyone and anyone because that was who he was — Bentley Harrington. I found her in an empty classroom; she was leaning against the far end table, nails slowly rhythmically tapping against the wooden surface.

I have never seen her with a bare face, nor did I think I ever will. Naked and exposed, she stood in front of me. I noticed the circles under her eyes — she looked as if she hadn't slept. Her hair was braided in single plait, green coloured eyes studied the ground as if there was something interesting.

"I don't know why I complied," she began the second the door closed behind me. "Why I allowed you to weasel your way into our group? I must admit that it was foolish on my half, but you... You were foolish to believe that you could trust someone here."

Languidly, she looked up, tormenting me with jade eyes, a rarity. Cocking her head to the side, her forehead creased when she frowned.

"I would've thought she'd taught you that. Scarlett always knew she couldn't trust anyone at Harrington, not even herself. Power is everything and our poor Red could not get enough of it."

"Power makes you sick, evil. You guys are twisted. The people here are afraid of you, afraid of this manipulative power you have over them," My insults meant nothing to her. There was a ghost of a smile playing on her lips.

"You're probably right," she stated. "But why make them love you, when they can fear you?"

"I know everything, Celeste," I threatened. "Everything. Your dirty little secrets are going to come out. You won't control Harrington anymore."

She observed me, studying my movements, my expressions, every inch of me did not go unnoticed by her. Celeste Leon looked exhausted, she looked like she didn't want to be standing in front of me, it was unmissable. Her shoulders were pushed back, she held her head high, emitting power and royalty, but the crown she bared was heavy and stained with blood. Eyes glanced away from me, she looked distant and lost.

"I wonder if you knew about her secrets, Candace? Would you look at her the same way?"

I frowned. "What are you talking about?"

"I don't understand why you have this image of her being an angel," she sighed. "She was anything but. Truth be said, she fit in perfectly with us."

I took a threatening step forward, glaring at the green-eyed beauty, "Don't you dare say that, she was nothing like you."

Celeste didn't look the slightest bit afraid, not saying anything as she studied me. Then, she chuckled mockingly, trying to fight the glee that masked her face but the smirk on her lips gave her away. She closed the distance that kept me safe away from her, towering over me in her 10inch heels, belittling me.

"How disappointing. I guess our princess Scarlett wasn't honest to her best friend for life," Her voice laced in venom. "How many lies has she told you, Candace? I'm curious. Why don't I tell you all my favourite moments, and then you can tell me if you still think she's any angel?"

My silence was enough for her to continue. She leaned back against a table; her arms crossed over her chest as she stood with her guards up. A sigh left her lips, taunting me with what I was hoping was lies.

"Scarlett loved the attention, she loved every second of it. It was never about wanting to ensure Harrington was ruled properly, whatever that meant.

It was always about her wanting what I had. She loved it, the popularity, the glamour, the illusion, the drugs and parties. Every second of it. In fact, she was made perfectly for this lifestyle. I'd never met someone who easily complimented us like her. She was ruthless, manipulative, cunning. I bet you didn't know that she slept with Bentley, Kaito, Elijah — although I don't think that was voluntary."

I snarled, "You disgust me."

The corner of her lips widened, she looked like a Cheshire cat. "Exactly what I said to Scarlett when I saw her leaving my boyfriend's house."

"She wouldn't have done that. She hated him, that doesn't make sense."

"Why would I lie about a dead girl?" Celeste scoffed. "God, I was furious. I wanted to snap her pretty little head off her body, but Bentley was fascinated with her — I wasn't allowed to touch her. Scarlett was not innocent. She slept with anyone who could give her a single taste of power, she'd chase after the rich, she 'd torment the weak.

"She was like us, Candace. The Scarlett you knew was dead the second she stepped into Harrington. You could say I respected her slightly, she had this burning passion to never not want more. She got want she wanted, it didn't matter who she betrayed or hurt.

"Did you know that Akari had a met up with this modelling company and Scarlett ripped that away from her? Even though it was brief, Madeline had found someone she generally adored and wanted to be with — Scarlett slept with him. She didn't stop at just that.

"She was so hungry for more, it was like a drug — the pills didn't kill her, it was her greed. Zane didn't love her, maybe like a sister but not romantically. Of course, the one person she wanted the most, she couldn't have. God, she was crazy. She went to such lengths to have him. It's actually funny thinking about it now."

"Why are you telling me this? My opinion on her won't change based on your words," I spat out.

"She was not a good person, Candace," Celeste snarled, her eyes blazing as if there were flames within them. "I just want you to know that whatever you're planning to do, isn't worth it. She's dead. It's not going to bring her back."

Squinting my eyes, I tilted my head to the side in bewilderment. "Why are you with him, Celeste?"

She looked taken back with my reply, most likely expecting me to argue back at her, but she looked like she didn't even want to say such things to me, like she wasn't doing this because she wanted to — she was doing it because she was forced it. A part of me felt sorry for her; trapped in a tower, guarded obsessively by a dragon, her freedom was snatched away from her the second she met Bentley, the moment their families agreed to marry the pair. Her right to say no or yes did not belong to her. Bentley had her on a leash, tormenting her.

"You don't know anything, Candace. Our world is so much more complicated that you think, and Scarlett knew that but her fascination in owning the power we bare, it killed her. She couldn't survive what we go through."

Although, her answer was vague, I understood what she meant but I refused to let sentiment get the best of me. She might be honest with me, but Celeste Leon always had a second motive, nothing she did or say did not benefit her. I released a shaky breath of air, breaking the spell of guilt and discomfort that suffocated me, ignoring my subconscious that told me to not go through with my plan; I stood up straighter, tucking a strand of blonde hair behind my ear, mustering up every ounce of courage I had left within me.

"I'm sorry that I don't understand your life or that I can't sympathise, but you and your friends had costed my best friend's life. I believe in justice, Celeste, and you believe in deception. I refuse to allow anyone follow the same path as Scar," I declared coldly.

"You believe in revenge, Candace," Her reply was instant, composed, like she'd been in this situation before. "There's not justice in this world. Only revenge."

"Maybe that's what you believe."

The flicker of annoyance in her eyes was enough for me to know that her patience was long gone. Straightening her spine, prim and proper, like she had been brought to act, her eyes narrowed down into slits that could've been mistaken for daggers. Her lips curled into a scowl, her green eyes became dangerously dark, the true illusion of Celeste Leon came in to play.

The visionary Queen of Harrington knew that she wasn't going to win, she couldn't change my mind. I could see her calculating her next move, her eyes flashing as she assessed the damage in the form of Candace Lowell. She couldn't lose, not when her future was on the line, not when it was Bentley pulling the strings — it was a risk she was not willing to take.

I waited to hear her words, words that acted like knives and bullets. I wanted to know what she was going to do to break me, to squash me between her sun kissed fingers like the ant I was. She was the Queen Bee, and in her hive, no one could do anything without her say. I was a threat. I wondered how Celeste dealt with threats. Silence basked us. It felt like hours until she spoke again, but it was only a couple of minutes — minutes that haunted me, and she knew it did.

"You loved her," Celeste stated.

I scowled, narrowing my eyes at her like she was mad. "Of course, I loved her. She was my best friend—"

"No," she interrupted with a scoff that sounded like a laugh as well, a smirk growing on her face that said it all; she won. "You loved her more than a friend, more than a best friend. That's why you're doing all of this, why you went to such lengths to destroy us: people who are untouchable."

My eyes were wide, processing her words as they settled over me, suffocating me like a thick blanket, words trapped in my throat. She chuckled darkly, running her fingers through her ebony hair as her cat eyes twinkled.

"Poor Candy. That's why you're doing all of this. Oh god, it makes so much more sense," Celeste raised a brow with amusement. "We ruined the person you loved so much; we took her away from you. What a joke. And do you know what the best part is?"

Coldness caressed my cheeks, making me aware of the tears that escaped. Tears that I had refused to give to her, tears which easily betrayed me, exposing my innermost feelings. My heart was beating rapidly, my palms sweaty and clenched into a tight fist as anger and hatred bubbled within me.

Celeste seemed satisfied but I knew her too well, she wanted to break me, destroy everything within me. And when she bent forward, green eyes coldly glaring at me contrasting the triumphant smirk on her coral lips, whispering her merciless words, she did.

"She never loved you back."

She broke me.

*

"I love you, Scarlett," I cried. I couldn't help it. I hated how she stared at me with uncaring, cold eyes. I hated how I couldn't tell what she was thinking. I hated how much I loved her. I hated myself. "Please, don't do this."

"I don't love you, Candace. Not anymore, not how you want me to," she responded. She sounded too much like Celeste Leon. I didn't who she was, the girl in front of me wasn't my best friend, but I fooled myself into believing she was.

"I saw it coming," I admitted brokenly. "But it still hurts. Because you never know when or how it will happen – you just know that it's going to." I blew out a breath, wiping away my tears, forcing the smile. She looked at me indifferently. "You try prepare for it, but you can't. It still feels like you've been stabbed. It tears you apart from the inside out, the knowing. And when it finally happens, you're ripped open all over again."

"I'm sorry," Her words were a whisper of insincerity, lies and broken promises.

"Don't be," I replied numbly. "You're not the girl I fell in love with."

I didn't wait to hear her voice, to give her the pleasure of owning the last words — no, I wanted that for myself. I gave her one last cold look before turning away, walking away from runaway where her jet patiently waited for her to board — I walked away from her.

"Miss Lowell, I hope you know that the attitude you are bringing to this academy is not acceptable," Principal Ashton said, breaking the haunting memory — my last memory of Scarlett. "May I ask what has brought this behaviour?"

"Candace has been going through a lot, Principal Ashton," My mother answered for me, hands on her lap, the firmness in her tone clearly showed how annoyed she was. "As you know, one of your students passed away last year."

Principal Ashton's face fell, sorrow glistening in her eyes. "Yes. Miss Lockwood, a brilliant asset to Harrington."

"Candace and Scarlett were best friends," My mother explained. Principal Ashton glanced at me pitifully, clasping her hands together. "Candace has been grieving and it has taken a large toll on her."

"With no disrespect, Miss Lowell, but why would you choose to attend Harrington?" the Principal asked me.

"Because, Scarlett told me it was the best school in the world," I responded emotionlessly.

"Nevertheless, was it the best decision to make?"

I didn't reply, swallowing inaudibly, my throat dry, my eyes trained onto the ground, refusing to look up. I was tired. Beyond tired in fact. Was it the best decision to make?

"I apologise for my daughter's behaviour, Principal Ashton. I can assure you that she'll refocus on her education and stay on top of her attendance. Grief can only last for some time, Candace is a bright girl and I believing coming to Harrington was the best decision made for my daughter—"

"No, it wasn't," I interrupted.

"Excuse me?" Mother outrageously asked.

My eyes flickered up. My mother stared at me with utter confusion, a splitting image of me — bright oceanic eyes, blonde curls that reached her shoulders unlike mine, hollowed features. It had been a while since I saw her, since we sat down for this long. I knew she met someone new; she thought I didn't hear she enter the house at 1 a.m. I wondered at what point did we lose our mother–daughter relationship, and when she started treating me like the Elites' parents.

"It was the wrong decision to make, Mother. I don't want to be here. Not when I'm still not over Scarlett. I can't stay here; I want to leave."

Her mother opened and closed like a fish, speechless and baffled. Of course, she would be. I was so enthusiastic to come here at the beginning of the academic year. Principal Ashton leaned forward, a small smile as her brown eyes glistened with understanding.

"Very well, Miss Lowell," she said. "It was wonderful to meet you and thank you for attending Harrington Preparatory."

*

Too much had happened in one day — Akari, Celeste, Principal Ashton — and now here I was clearing out my locker, tucking my belonging into my Prada bag. The corridors were empty, lessons had started a while back, and I wanted to leave as soon as possible — the mere thought of being here for a second longer tore me apart. Every step I'd take away from the lavish building was a step to a fresh start; I could almost breathe in the air of freedom. Scarlett would want that for me. I wanted that for me.

I don't think I was going to miss sitting with Elites whilst the entire school idolised you, or partying at the hottest locations, or eating at extravagant restaurants and cafes. I never wanted to experience such a lifestyle again. It was toxic, it contaminated your bloodstream, your mind and morals. Poison, that's what they were.

The Elites didn't need someone like me or Scarlett to break them, they could do it easily to themselves — a set of self-destructive group of friends. Fake smiles, dark secrets, treacherous lies; the Elites were a building without stable foundation.

They'd topple over soon enough, in time when the truth revealed itself. I walked down the corridor one last time, pausing in front of Akari's locker. I contemplated what to do before quickly grabbing a pen and paper, scribbling a note.

You know, I really did see you as a friend. You're not innocent, you played a role, but you deserve better than the Elites, than Bentley. Don't get caught up in the lifestyle because it will kill you. They're toxic, I wished you listened to me.

I'm leaving for good, it's for the best. Although, I didn't have the courage to complete what Scarlett began, I really hope you do. It's never too late to do the right thing, Akari. I sent the copy of the file to your email — it's the last copy.

I wish you the best.

Candace.

Folding the piece of paper, I slipped it into the cracks of the locker. It took me a long minute before I moved away, glancing down the corridor one last time. Memories flashed as quick as the speed of light, every second and every moment. Zane's grey eyes haunted me, and I know they would for a long time.

I squeezed my eyes together, forcing the memories to burn away from my mind, the good and the bad. I clutched onto my bag tightly, strutting down the empty halls once I gathered my thoughts. I wasn't sure if Scarlett would be appalled or proud, I wasn't sure who won and who lost. I don't think I wanted to know.

If I did, it would torment me. And, although questions were let unanswered, scandals left unrevealed, I did know that I could no longer live in the past.

The Elites probably didn't learn their lesson, they probably won't ever learn. But at least they know that their secrets can never be buried forever, that there would always be someone to dig the skeletons out their graves, that no matter the wealth or status they bared — there will always be someone who can play the game better than them. Whether it was the

Elites, or it was me who claimed checkmate, it didn't matter because in the end, all that was left was shards of heartbreak and rubbles of amity.

Thus, when the mahogany doors closed behind me, I closed the past, kissing Harrington goodbye.

-

The end?

- fariha.

18 | in her wake

Chapter XIII: In her wake

INFORMATION WAS POWER. To have information was to have power. And, in Akari's hand, she had the power to destroy what should've never have started. A part of her wished Candace didn't leave, it felt like she lost yet another friend, but for most part, she was glad. Harrington was noxious. It took Akari long enough to recognise that. Something had shifted in Harrington over the past days, the environment had changed dramatically.

The news of Candace's relationship with Scarlett was the hottest topic of the week, the students of Harrington buzzed with gossip and whispers. Kaito's confused expression when he heard the news of Candace's departure was still imprinted in Akari's mind; information he didn't know first. Elijah's fingers worked quickly whilst he typed, mulling over the fact that Candace knew everything — he wasn't sure what that meant for him.

Peering over his laptop, he noticed that Akari's eye kept glancing at her phone as she twiddled her fingers — a sign of unease. He wondered why. Zane stormed into the cafeteria, his grey eyes wide and lost — he looked broken and battered. Her breath hitched when he stared at her. She knew what he wanted to know. Even in unspoken words, she knew what he was going to say. Moving her head delicately, his face fell, his shoulders slouched before he disappeared out the doors.

"What's going on?" Celeste asked, hands entwined with her boyfriend, as the pair took their rightful seats. For a fleeting moment, Bentley stared at Akari with the sudden urge to kiss her, to hold her instead of the girl with green eyes. But he wouldn't dare. Captivated by his murky eyes, words failed Akari as she neglected to answer Celeste's question.

Elijah's brows knitted together. "Candace pulled out of Harrington."

Celeste didn't speak for a minute, cocking her head to the side before a slow, deadly smirk graced her coral lips.

"Took her long enough."

*

She waited for him during lunch, leaning against his locker. His bleak, brown eyes haunted with ghosts and deceits found her in the crowd, examining her body as if she was an object, his play toy. Her fragile features, petite and feline, attracted him to her, enticing him. She was a temptation, a sin, his forbidden secret and his darkest desire. She knew that.

"We need to speak," Akari ordered. He never smiled, not unless he found something entertaining, but Bentley only found satisfaction in twisted things.

Staring at her a lengthy, suspenseful minute, he nodded. "Very well."

The classroom they entered was empty, quiet, far from peeking eyes and curious gossipers — Akari couldn't risk Celeste finding out about this interaction. She hated Akari enough and by having such a risky conversation at school would only add fuel to that hatred, tantalizing her to release those disgraceful photos and videos to the public eye.

"What is it you want?" he asked, tone level and unbothered.

He observed every movement she made, every inch of her body, every flicker of emotion. She loathed it when he did that. It affected her; her bones trembled at the sight of him, and not because she was scared, but rather out of desire.

She hated herself for loving a monster like him, she hated for doting someone who was promised to another, she hated herself, but mostly she hated how she knew she'd never have a future with him, and yet she always hoped she would. A large part of her pitied Celeste, she never understood their relationship, but she knew it was far too lethal.

Although, Celeste was the epitome of an evil queen, at the same time, she was a locked-up princess, guarded by the riches and manipulation of the Harrington's'. Maybe that's why Celeste was so vindictive; she was angry, broken and hurt, therefore she expressed it out on everyone else.

"I want — No, I wanted you. I've always wanted you but, now, I don't think I that is true anymore," Akari began, brushing the specks of dust on her tartan skirt.

Bentley knitted his brow. "Was that all?"

"Will you ever tell her?"

The frown entrenched on his face visibly deepened. His forehead creased as his eyes narrowed. "Why would I repeat what she already knows?"

For the longest time, Akari stared at him — not out of fascination or infatuation, but out of sympathy and guilt. He had everything he could ever want with the snap of his fingers, but he would never have someone who truly loved him. Akari was another leaf on his branch, swaying side to side until she fell hard, until he was bored. But, Celeste, she was a vine; entwined tightly around his branches, with roses blossoming and thorns prodding.

"I can't do this anymore," she sighed, running her fingers through her mahogany locks.

"I didn't realise there was something going on the first place."

His tone was sharp, indifferent, impatient. She scoffed, crossing her arms over her chest as she rested against the teacher's desk.

"Why do you always do this? Act like you don't care, like what happened between us didn't exist. I don't get it. You hate seeing me happy with someone other than you, you come running to my aid when anything happens. I know you love me, Bentley, so why do you pretend that I'm not standing on front of you?"

"If you're having a tantrum, please have it to someone else. This is such a waste of my time," he said frostily.

Akari's jaw flexed, gritting her teeth together as she wrestled hard to keep her wrath a bay. Her hands balled into a tight fist, the urge to punch him was irresistible, and the ironic thing was that he was daring her. His eyes gleamed. She didn't want to give him the satisfaction, if that was the only thing she hasn't given, she refused to do it now. A sigh escaped her plump lips as she ran her hand over her face.

"I've given you everything. I kept hoping I could convince you that I was worth it, worth more than 'just talking' to, but I can't," She looked him in the eyes, her gaze a mixture of tears and steel. "I told myself you'd come around, but you haven't. And, deep down, I knew you wouldn't, but I kept trying. I thought it would be too hard to give up on you."

"Akari—" Bentley disrupted but she held a hand up, silencing him with the sharpest of action. Akari took a deep breath in like she could breathe oxygen for the first time; it had tasted differently, like liberty.

"But here I am, giving up on you, and, honestly, it's more of a relief than anything. So, now I'm going to walk away, and I'm not going to look back. But I know you're going to regret it, even if it's just for a moment."

She didn't wait to hear his seductive words based on false promises, or how he'd reach out to her, his fingertips brushing gently against her skin, and somehow convince her that there was a future. She didn't want to hear his lies.

Akari loved him, and she knew, even if it's for a while, she always would, but, at least for now, the love diminished like a candle in the wind. And, she left the classroom holding snugly onto that feeling because she knew if she looked back, she'd regret her decisions even if it's for a feeble second, it would be enough for her to run back into his callous, forbidden arms.

*

Zane felt betrayed.

She left without saying goodbye, without a reason or an explanation. She disappeared like the smoke to his cigarettes. It was as if she never existed. But her presence left a stain on the group, a change that brought discomfort to the people he once called his friends. There was a hole in his heart, a hole that she had stolen, a hole that only she could fill. It took him a while to realise what he felt towards her, but by the time he knew, it was too late.

She slipped right out of her fingertips. She vanished into thin air. He leaned against his car, a wealthy, lavish car his father bought him as a gift due to his acceptance to Columbia — a university that was wrongfully given to him. He lingered. Watching his fellow students scuffle out the building, rushing to their town cars or luxurious limos, he observed each one of them until he caught the one, he wanted.

"Clermont," he called out. Even though there was quite a distance, Zane saw how cautious Harris was as he looked up. "We need to speak."

The boys sat on a bench in the empty Central Park, ignoring the frosty weather, the cold biting against their skin — it was hard to tell whether it was cold because of the weather of because of the situation. Zane studied Harris; his hair was like onyx, spilling past his eyes, covering coffee eyes which were down casted, a mocha overcoat covered his broad shoulders, protecting him from the chilly weather. He was the closest person to both Scarlett and Candace — he betrayed them both.

"Why did you betray Scar?" Zane asked, a question he'd been wondering for over a year.

"Bentley said my sister's life was on the line," Harris responded, exhaling heavily. "I was torn, but I couldn't let my sister get hurt because of Scar's unhealthy obsession."

"So, what about Candace?"

"Madeline."

Zane blew out a breath, running his frostbitten finger through his shaggy hair.

"Who has the files?"

The words tumbled out of his mouth before he could stop himself. He didn't want to know the answers. Harris' eyes flickered into the distance at the sound of a little girl laughing, the corner of his lips quirking up; he remembered when his little sister was that vivacious and cheerful.

"Akari," he replied.

The name that bared the responsibility that cost Scarlett's life and Candace's mentality. The name that held the key to whether justice would be served or not. Anticipation greeted Harris, he wondered what the Japanese girl's next move would be. She had the power, the control, the choice to do the right thing or the wrong thing — it was hard to tell the difference between the two.

*

There was always a moment in Celeste Leon's life where she'd wish she had never met Bentley Harrington. Today was one of those days. Frustratingly enough, what Candace had asked played incessantly in her mind like a broken record.

Why was she with him?

To outsiders, it appeared so simple, the answer was only three words. But, to Celeste, it was more than three words; it was a story, a long and complicated tale that didn't have an ending where she'd be happy, no matter how many times she changed the plot. She hated to admit it, but she was jealous of Candace. Even though, she spun a web of lies, somewhere along the line she'd caught Zane, and, despite knowing the truth, he still loved her.

For Celeste, on the other hand, rather than being caught in the web, she was wrapped in the spider's silk, suffocated and lost any sense of freedom. The smallest notion of such treacherous behaviour amused Celeste; the corner of her lips didn't reach her eyes like it used.

The halls were empty, the final bell had rung, and everyone had rushed home in excitement of the weekend to come. She propped against her locker, her back marginally arched as she admired her acrylic nails. She was waiting. Waiting for her knight in cold, steeled armour. Waiting to be taken back to her fortress.

Bentley loved the way she dressed herself for him: plaid skirt hiked up far above her knee, black stockings matched with those Louboutin's he gifted her on her birthday, and those wicked coral lips. He loved the idea of her. There was a smirk as sinister as his soul that played on his lips at the sight of her. Their love was cruel and twisted, some wouldn't even be sure to call it love. Like toys, they played with each until they got bored. In this case, Celeste was the only one bored.

"Waiting for me?" he asked rhetorically.

He knew the answer, he just enjoyed seeing the look of dislike on her face even if it's for a split second; he relished in it. Without waiting for an answer, he leaned forward and captured her lips, gripping her waist. Brutal, rough and uncaring, glacial against her flushed features.

Celeste couldn't expect any less from Bentley, it was just like him — a businessman at heart, controlling even his most intimate interactions. Her hand snaked under his jacket, wrapping around his back, and dug her nails across his cotton shirt to draw him closer as she fervently kissed him back.

It was sick — their love. Both sadistically and masochistically sick. However, today would be the last. The second she felt like she couldn't breathe, like her the oxygen level within her was critical, she shoved him away. Her breathing was laboured as she inhaled heavily whilst his thumb rubbed the lipstick off his lips, the marking she left. He reviled being marked.

"How comes you're waiting today?" Bentley inquired, fixing his blazer and straightening out his tie. "Don't you need to prepare for tonight?"

"Tonight will not happen," Celeste promised, her voice thick with the battered confidence from the years of being labelled as Bentley's girlfriend — that's all she ever was.

"And why is that?" A brow lifted; his eyes sparkled in merriment.

"Because we are over."

For the longest time, he spoke no words nor made any type of action. The words hovered densely above them; it didn't sit well with her. Then, his head tilted to the side, there was no longer an essence of amusement on his face. His eyes were dark like the night, his face chilly like ice, features that she once found attractive now caused hostile tremors to rattle down her spine.

Bentley exhaled — irritated and unsurprised. Why would he be? This was the nth time she tried to break up with him, and the times where he'd allow her to free herself from his shackles, he found that she'd run back to him in less than a week. Old habits die hard. Albeit, this time seemed to be different.

She appeared fed up, tired and depressed like all the other times, but there was a dangerous spark in her eyes which he knew full well that it meant she was going to fight until her last breath. Now, Bentley didn't want that to happen; he wasn't in the mood to amuse her.

"No."

"What?"

"I said, no."

He shoved his hands into the depths of his pockets, turning away and striding down the halls. He didn't get very far as her ivory hands snaked out and clasped his wrist, forcing him to face her. Her eyes blazed like fire, the flame that he had weakened suddenly reignited and burned brighter than ever before.

"I don't care what you say, Bentley," she hissed, determined to get her way. "We are breaking up."

He pushed her hand off him, glaring furiously at her. Bentley was in disbelief. Where did this sudden confidence come from? Who did she think she was? He was livid.

"Why?" It was an uncomplicated question, yet it held a thousand of tacit emotions, opaque with dominance and anger.

"I'm done with you, Bentley. Done with your games and how you treat me," she spat venomously. "This is stupid what we are doing, I don't even understand what we actually are doing. You don't love me anymore, not like you used to; I can see it by the way you look at me with sheer disgust. I'm sick of it and I'm not dealing with it any longer."

"This is a joke," he chuckled darkly.

"I know about your little conversation with Akari. Even she knew you weren't worth it anymore, and it took her damn well long enough to realise."

Something in Bentley awoken at the sound of the Japanese girl's name. The beast within him growled territoriality, the name that rolled off Celeste's tongue showed her disdain evidently. His features hardened as his jaw flexed whilst he struggled to calm his temper, listening to the girl he was promised to.

"You clearly love her. Don't think I haven't seen the way you stare at her, or how concerned you get about her. It's sickening," Celeste sneered, her lips coiled in irritation. Her attitude infuriated him; his patience snapped.

"Whether I love her or not, it doesn't matter because she'll never give me what I want," he snarled, frosty, slim fingers curling around her wrist and yanking her towards him. "And what I want, Celeste, is power. With you, by my side, we both can have all the power in the world. We'd be invincible, Celeste. We'd have all the riches and jewels possible; you'd live the life you've dreamt of having since you were a girl. So, stop acting childish and talking bullshit about breaking up, and fix your act."

Every syllable spoken held venomous resentment towards the girl in front of him, unaffected by how her big, green eyes watered with tears.

"You are going to stand by my side tonight, on that podium, and we are going to announce our engagement. Do you understand, Celeste?"

The flicker within her diminished, a single blow was all she needed to be burnt out. Bentley was the dragon and she was the imprisoned princess — never to be free, never to be happy. The crown she bared came with a price, hefty and poisonous, Celeste knew that. She swallowed coarsely, shrugging off his hold, eyes trained onto the ground as she battled her tears.

"I hate you so much."

"I don't care if you hate me, if you'll never forgive me or if you don't love me. I don't care," he spoke, much more evenly than before. His voice levelled yet basked in dominance. "We weren't raised to learn to love one another, we were taught to rule. I won't give you love, but I can give you the world, Celeste. You'd be nothing without me."

He left Celeste; hand stucked into the pocket as he strolled down the corridor of Harrington Preparatory. Celeste glimpsed up, glowering into his retreating back when, fromthe corner of her eye, she spotted the Japanese girl, clutching her books against her chest as she observed the scene with torment, tears tainting her cheeks. Curling her fingers into a fist, Celeste clamped her jaw as she glaredat the girl, obscuring the grieve with anger and abhorrence.

Thus, in that moment, she never hated anyone more.

19 | the girl with the pink lips

Turn your face to the sun and the shadows will fall behind you.

[New Zealander Proverb]

Epilogue: The girl with the pink lips

I SAT NERVOUSLY in Elan; an aesthetically beautiful cafe situated in Mayfair. My fingers drummed against my knee as I waited, my anxiety suddenly increasing. The weather was warm, the sun beaming outside brightly, it was a wonderful day to meet an old friend. I was apprehensive, speculating how she'd look after four months.

A part of me was disappointed that she never took the initiative to do the right thing, but I wasn't surprised, nor did I care. Leaving Harrington meant I left the responsibility of that file, therefore it no longer concerned me. Whether she'd expose the Elites, or she'd burn the last remaining evidence of their scandalous secrets, didn't matter to me.

My lips suddenly felt dry, so I hastily grabbed a compact mirror and lip gloss to tend to it. Flipping the mirror open, I delicately applied the pink stained gloss across my lips as I admired my reflection, my cheeks no longer hollow, my skin much lighter and clearer, my cerulean eyes vibrant — I looked like myself. Not Scarlett, Celeste or someone popular; I was me.

My phone buzzed on the table, catching my eyes where I read the message from my therapist about next week's session whilst I tucked my items away in a Valentino bag. When I left New York, I made the courageous decision to have a one on one with a therapist, to finally get over my grieving; I didn't comprehend how much of a toll Scarlett's death had disturbed me. Acute eating disorder, high anxiety and psychotic depression. I guess it was an eye opening.

A bell chimed, my eyes flicking in the same direction. Akari walked in gracefully: her radiant hair cut just below her shoulders, and her features looked healthier whilst her eyes twinkled perkily. She wore a pastel blue dress, adorned with nude Prada heels and purse, complimented with a simple silver necklace.

Keeping contact with Akari was a decision I had made gradually after she forgave me; I missed her and realised how much her friendship was precious to me. She had messaged me a couple days back, informing me about her layover in London and asked to meet up. With a high-pitched squeal, she rushed over to where I was sitting, besides the flower wall.

"I missed you," she exclaimed, hugging me across the table. I giggled softly, embracing her back. "Oh god, it's been ages. How are you?"

Settling into our seats, I grinned at the Japanese girl. "Great actually. I enrolled in King Alfred's and I accepted the offer in Oxford; I'm heading up there this August. I think I'm in a good place. How have you been?"

The smile she gave me reached her ears, her eyes crinkling, "I've been really good. I've been focusing a lot on my music and decided to move back to Japan this summer after I'm done travelling — there was so much I haven't seen yet. Also, after you left, I finally ended whatever me and Bentley had. It took me long to realise that he never loved me like I did him, he loved the control and game."

"I'm sorry, Akari," I murmured, sympathetically placing my hand over hers.

She shook her head; the smile never fell. "Don't be. They were going to be engaged, I wasn't going to be someone's mistress."

"I'm proud of you, Akari. I know you loved him a lot, I can't imagine how much this must've hurt."

"I think you do know," she replied oddly.

I frowned. "What do you mean?"

Her mouth opened to respond but, as if everything was in slow motion, Zane Stryker strolled in, one hand in his pocket whilst the other held his phone against his ear as he spoke with an apprehensive expression.

His jaw was more refined than the last time I has seen him, his cheekbones had risen a tad. His hair style was different, the length trimmed, and the side shaved so he had an undercut, exposing his vivid silver eyes. About 20 odd people was captivated by his beauty, their eyes flickering to his direction whilst he ordered at the counter.

I swallowed drily; my words lodged in my throat especially seeing him in a navy suit — he didn't look like the Zane I once knew. Tucking away his phone, he looked up, my heart pounding against my chest. The world came to a stop when our eyes met, like there was nothing in between us. Suddenly, all those memories came rushing back and the feelings I buried deep within me were revived the second the corner of his lips lifted.

"I brought him along with me. He needed a ride because he had a meeting, so I offered," Akari whispered. "You guys left it on a bad note, and I think at least one of us deserves a happy ending."

I broke my gaze away from the silver eyed boy, focusing my attention onto her. Her head leaned to the side, her gaze tender and feline. The guilt and sadness I had tucked away came gushing back, but, as if she knew, Akari daintily shook her head.

"When you gave me that file, I spent days wondering what to do. Then, I saw Celeste and Bentley. It was almost reflexive, but I deleted it off my phone. Not because I was afraid of the consequences but because that would never reverse what had happened. She wasn't going to come back; Bentley wasn't going to love me, and the file could easily be fixed by PR specialists. I can't justify my actions or make you understand, but I knew it would open wounds; wounds that were healing and leave scars instead," Akari sighed. "Elijah is getting what he deserved. His trial has been going on for a few months, more and more girls keep coming forward. I couldn't let him get away with it. I was stupid to tell Scarlett to ignore what had happened, I didn't consider how much it affected her. It was selfish."

"Akari—"

"I told dad what Kaito's been doing, he was pretty mad. I don't think I'll be seeing him for some time," She propped forward, clasping my hands. "And, Zane didn't take the offer at Columbia."

I was about to speak when Zane closed the distance between him and us, disrupting my train of thoughts. Akari sent me a cheeky grin and wink before she slipped into the restroom without another word. Awkwardly, he paused beside the table whilst I nervously gathered myself, but my feelings were all over the place. I was a mess and he hadn't even said a single word to me yet.

"Can I take a seat?" he asked carefully. I nodded mindlessly, looking every-where other than at him. "You look different."

His voice was deep like the ocean and I felt like I was sinking. I hated how he had the biggest effect on me even though I hadn't seen him for months. Daringly, I peeked up, my breath hitching when he gave me a small smile.

"Good or bad?" The words tumbled out of my mouth before I even knew it.

"Good different. You look happier."

"I am happier."

"I'm glad."

The silence engulfed us as we both got lost in the depths of each other's eyes. My throat felt parched, my heart hammered against my ribs, my cheeks flushed under his scorching gaze and my ears burned in embarrass-ment. I didn't know what to say or what to do. How can we walk away from what tied us together in the first place?

I wasn't sure if he was asking the same question as his eyebrows furrowed together, and his forehead creased. I was restlessly fiddling with my fingers on the table when he reached out and encased them into his warm, firm hands. Sparks erupted within me, fireworks and sparklers, the mere touch of him brought an overwhelming sense of happiness to my heart. I felt like a little girl all over again.

"I never got to apologise," he spoke gently. "For everything you went through. We caused a lot of pain, the damage we did was inexcusable. I'm sorry."

"The past is the past," I mumbled. "We can't keep living like in it, we can only move forward."

Over the last few months, it was something I had learnt, something I had to teach myself. I couldn't go back no matter how much I wished I could, nor could I change what had happened. I couldn't see the future or rewrite it, but I could live in the moment. And, I did. Every day after leaving that lavish building in the expensive city and far from the wealthy upper–class socialites, I spent catching up on time I missed — time that I spent wasted on revenge.

"I've missed you, Candace," he whispered. "I wish you didn't leave before I could tell you how I felt."

I closed my eyes, moving my hands away from his captivity. The barriers I spent months building around my true feelings had started to crack, shattering bit by bit, shard by shard until they were just pieces of broken fragments.

"Zane—"

"I love you, Candace. I have for some time. I'm sorry it had taken me this long to be honest."

The words I so desperately wanted say were trapped in my throat. I love you. I have always loved you. They refused to escape my lips, as if it was a secret. But this wasn't a secret I wanted to keep to myself. I wanted to tell him, I had to tell him. Every fibre in my body burned at the sight of him, memories flashing until they came to one — our first kiss.

My fingertip touched my lips as I opened my eyes; I didn't even realise I was doing it. I could still feel the warmth, how he had shrouded me in heat despite the night being very cold, or how he'd given me tingles from head to toe. His silvery eyes observed me carefully, waiting for a reply.

"I love..."

I hesitated, ducking my head down in fear of witnessing the look of dejection across his godlike face. But then, I felt his soft hands, delicately touching mine with reassurance that reflected in his eyes when I had peered up.

"It's okay," His voice silky and quiet, the smile on his face assured me he wasn't upset. "Do you think we can have a fresh start?"

Time had repaired a lot of things, and one of them was my capability to let people in. I had forgiven Akari, she had made mistakes, she was only human. I forgave the fact that Scarlett wasn't perfect; she wasn't the person I painted her to be. I forgave myself. The guilt that gnawed within me and the repetitive thought that I could've saved her, I had let it go. Forgiveness was the first stage to moving on.

So, removing any ounce of fear or uncertainty, I answered, "I'd like that."

His lips widened into the most magnificent grin, setting butterflies free, drowning me in the abyss of his silver eyes. And, I did not care one bit. One of his hand tenderly tucked a stray hair behind my ear, before cupping the side of my face, my eyes fluttering closed at the sensation of his heated touch.

There was still a long way to go, a bridge that we had to cross, to earn each other's trust once again. Nevertheless, the feeling of his touch had encouraged me that this was the start of a new beginning, a new era, a symbol that all things broken could also be repaired. I wasn't sure how he did it, but I felt something within me mending, healing.

We could finally try this the right way. No lies, deception or manipulation. A blank chapter, a new start. The heat disappeared and I tentatively opened my eyes to see Zane sticking his hand out, the corner of my pink lips curling into an amused smile.

"Hey, I'm Zane Stryker," he introduced warmly. "And you are?"

"Candace Lowell," I responded, shaking his hand, sparks exploded at the interaction. "It's a pleasure to meet you."

My smile broadened when he pressed his lips against my ivory skin, whilst I unwittingly fell in love once again, lost in the intensity of his silver gaze.

His eyes twinkled. "It's a pleasure to meet you too."

-

the making of the elites.

BEHIND THE STORY

THE ELITES IS A NOVELLA, largely inspired by Gossip Girl, Clique Bait, and Thirteen Reason Why, revolving around a transfer student who has moved to New York, to get revenge on the upper-class socialites of Manhattan, for the downfall of her best friend in the previous year. Based in the Upper East, a location famously known for its wealthy residents and lavish shops, The Elites focuses on the lifestyle of the most important, richest, people at Harrington Preparatory and how their inconsiderate behaviours can affect those around them negatively.

Throughout the novel, there are nine characters, who are mentioned mainly through the viewpoint of the protagonist, Candace. These nine characters, seven of whom belong to the 'Elites', all act as secondary characters, either helping or foiling Candace's plans. As one of my inspiration was Thirteen Reasons Why, I had included elements of sexual harassment, psychological abuse, drug abuse and solely, bullying, alongside other topics

– societal issues that aren't spoken enough about, and yet, occurs frequently within communities across the globe. Thus, I wanted to bring awareness about these subjects and had mentioned them within the novel as I believe that they hold great importance.

The main storyline was through the eyes of Candace Lowell, a student that has transferred from abroad to Harrington Preparatory, a private school situated in Manhattan. During the novel, Candace ventured through a journey to ruin a large group of friends, nicknamed 'Elites', and discovered their secrets that would ruin their future – vindictive for the way they had treated her best friend, Scarlett Lockwood. The genres I had chosen were romance, drama and thriller as the novel entailed romantic relationships, the tension between friends and the suspense of the unknown.

Regarding location, the novel takes place in New York City, a northern state in the U.S.A. The state was the best location for where the novel would take place as it's well known for its wealthy background. It accumulates up to $3 million of private wealth, being one of the richest cities in the world. In fact, most famously known, Manhattan, one of the five boroughs of NYC, is the wealthiest area in New York. I was also inspired by where Gossip Girl, by Cecily von Ziegesar, was located – the Upper East Side. It's largely known to be the home to the City's elite residents, well-known prep schools and designer boutiques.

It had acted as the perfect location for where The Elites would take place as it would not only exaggerate the wealth of the characters but also their power – a subject that is consistently brought up within the novel. The Upper East Side is identical with old money and classic New York sophistication, the mirror image of what the characters would portray.

The 'Elites' consisted of seven members: Celeste Leon, Bentley Harrington, Madeline Vos, Akari and Kaito Takahashi, Elijah Astor, and lastly, Zane Stryker. These seven characters played a vital role in Scarlett's downfall, the reason why Candace wanted revenge, and throughout the novel pieces of the past are revealed until one of the very few last chapters, where the entire story was disclosed.

Each member of the Elites is closely linked to the Seven Deadly Sins, cardinal sins that are a concept taught in Christianity; behaviours classified under the category if they give birth to other immoralities. The idea behind this was inspired by Inspector Calls, a morality play with themes circulating the Seven Deadly Sins. By linking these immoralities to the Elites, it had personified these sins and given the characters a strong explanation behind their personality.

When developing the characters, it was essential to give each character, especially the Elites, an authentic, and antique surname/name as it only amplified their appearance and the authority they have, hence, 'Harrington', 'Astor', 'Madeline', etc. There was also the element of culture, especially as three of the characters were neither English nor American. Leon and Takahashi had given the characters a different background, promoting diversity within the book.

RegardingCandace and Scarlett's relationship, I had to ensure that I did not reveal toomuch about their past to not ruin the suspense, but enough tounderstand Candace's desire for vengeance. Scarlett was never explicitly-mentioned throughout the novel and was only seen through the memories of Candace,which therefore created an image of mystery about her past.

Throughout the plot, it was never clearly revealed her current situation. One of the mostimportant elements in The Elites was the character development ofCandace. In the beginning, she was seen to be collected and revengeful, withthis well-thought master plan, mirroring the appearance Scarlett once had withthe 'red lips'. Then, during the middle, her emotions were spiralling out ofcontrol, her need to get vengeance was heightened as she began to act veryimpulsively.

However, by the end of the novel, Candace had detached herselffrom the grief that haunted her, allowing herself to be rid of guilt as shefinally came to term with the everything had happened. Instead of trying to besomeone popular, Candace was just herself and ready to move away from the past,hence the 'pink lips'. Throughout the course of the novel, it is unknown to thereaders that Candace is struggling with grief, facing difficulties to get overthe passing of her best friend. Behind her manipulative plans and deception,she was grieving, struggling to accept the condition her best friend was inand, because of this, she then faced delusions and hallucinations – symptoms ofpsychosis.

Psychosis is a type of mental health problem that causes people to perceive or interpret things around them differently. The two primary symptoms are delusions – where one has a strong belief not shared by others – and hallucinations - where a person hears, sees and, in some cases, feels, smells or tastes things that are not there.

There are other mental health problems such a severe depression that cause psychosis, however, it can also be triggered by other factors such as a traumatic experience and stress. It was seen that she was struggling with a lot of anxiety and pressure. It was not until chapter 11 where she meets the 'ghost' of Scarlett, which shows how much the stress, alongside grief, has affected her.

The physical interaction in future chapters between Scarlett and Candace aimed to cause confusion which was eventually explained at the end. There were connotations related to death that were linked to Scarlett such as 'black dress' or 'cold and icy', implicitly exposing Scarlett's situation.

Overall, the relationship between Scarlett and Candace was much more complicated than meets the eye, and it's eventually revealed that Candace had a deeper emotion towards Scarlett – unrequited love. Candace idolised Scarlett and showed signs of envy when Scarlett's attention was not on her but on someone else – this acted as a deeper meaning to Candace's thirst for vengeance, which was seen as she continuously reminds herself who she was doing this for.

The novel begins with "hello" she said with a sugary smile that would've seemed fake if she didn't have a branding of the high school sweetheart, but I had my doubts' as I had planned on demonstrating the distrustful attitudes seen throughout the story. The beginning intended on being powerful and gripping, in a way where the readers would question the entrance of this girl. Although, it wasn't known who this girl was until later, the fact that Candace already doubted her demonstrated the deceitful location in which the novel takes place, setting the scene for later chapters.

Equally, the novel did not have a definite ending, open to interpretation which was the approach I intended on taking. It finished with Zane and Candace forgiving each other, with little mention of other characters, but the ending was important to show character development, hence the chapter names for the preface and epilogue. 'The girl' has always been Candace but the switch from 'with red lips' to 'with pink lips' validated the growth and change of character from who she was at the beginning to the end.

The structure of the novella includes a text, formatted in how messages look in real life, from either Candace or Scarlett at the beginning of each chapter. It's the only source of interaction that would be seen consistently between the best friends, acting as a teaser for what the chapter might entail. The texts acted as an illusion that Scarlett was still alive and well, but in actuality, revealed in chapter 16, it's just Candace's attempt to stay connected with Scarlett, a sign of grief and psychosis.

During the novel, there were brief extracts of flashbacks that were solely based around Candace and Scarlett; the purpose of these flashbacks was to give context or foreshadow events. There were chapters which were in third person point of view, allowing readers to understand scenarios and emotions at the time from the perspective of all characters, to comprehend them more deeply within the novel, to engage with the characters by creating an emotional connection – whether it was negative or not.

As the novel was portrayed through the eyes of Candace, it aimed to get the readers to feel sympathetic towards Candace and her cause, to understand why she was acting in the way she was as they spent so much time in her 'brain'. The first-person narrative helped give logic and motivations to the character's that would seem otherwise evil, immoral or otherwise not relatable. It was essential for the readers to understand where Candace was coming from on her journey for vengeance.

Common themes throughout the novel were power and revenge. Power was seen in almost every chapter as it was necessary to emphasise how power can be abused. In modern-day society, people who have power and/or are in a position of responsibility, often abuse the power that had been given to them. It can never be sure that they are doing what's the best for those they're responsible for, but, more than often, they usually do what is best for them.

The Elites are meant to portray corruptive power, how it is easily abused and used to mistreat those they perceive as inferior. People who usually crave power often belittles and humiliates those around, for example during chapter 8. This was a theme that recurred during the entire novel, demonstrating how power can give 'high' similar to a drug, and used in malevolent ways. Another important theme was revenge, which was seen throughout the novel, particularly in Candace and Celeste. Both characters have the urge to get revenge on someone else. Whilst both characters have different reasons for vengeance, the intentions remain the same.

Furthermore, during the novel, Candace began to share similar traits to Celeste, such as manipulation, because the obsession with vengeance had overtaken her morals. There was also an important reference to the colour red, which was seen throughout the novel. Red is representative of emotions that are passionate, energetic and active – one of which is revenge. Throughout the novel, the connotations of red refer to the burning desire to having revenge and the anger felt by the main character but also refers back to Scarlett, who'd associated herself with the colour red.

The Elites were to bring alight subjects people tend to shy away from. I wanted to demonstrate that these issues can occur anywhere, so it didn't matter where the novel took place as these are worldwide issues, rather than national. Bullying is thought to not be common, when in fact, 20% of US students from age 12 to 18 are subject to bullying (2017) worldwide. Approximately 30% of US students have admitted to bullying others during a survey. This astounding statistic shows that, even in many recent years, many people are still victims of bullying, whether it's verbal or physical.

InThe Elites, bullying was a common theme as the exclusive group of friends abuse the power they have, belittling those around them and submitting them to humiliation. It was a subject very personal to me, and therefore, I had wanted to raise awareness that it's still very common. Whether it's being initiated by those with 'higher' status or not, it gives the inflictor this sense of 'authority' and 'power' afterwards.

Many people believe that bullying can be easily sorted if people had the courage to speak up when in fact, in a 2006 ABC article, it was seen that a school had ignored bullying, therefore being taken to court by five girls who had spoken up about their experience. Situations such as this are largely the reason why many do not speak up, therefore continuing to be subjected to bullying, in fear that these issues would be dismissed as minor and short-term problems.

TheElitesventured through several types of societal issues such as sexual assault todrug abuse, topics that aren't spoken publicly about as it thought to be ataboo, or people are uncomfortable. Hence why Thirteen Reasons Why was alarge inspiration during the development of this novel, as they mention a rangeof issues such a rape, substance abuse and most importantly bullying, and theeffects on the victims. In The Elites, Scarlett was subjective to thesematters, which had driven her to the edge and resulted in her death. As avictim of bullying, sexual assault and drug abuse, Scarlett was a characterthat had played the role of victims in all cases.

Sexual assault was particularly important in the novel, as seen in chapter 10/11/15, since it's unbelievably common within places of work and education – almost two-thirds of college students experience sexual harassment. However, 68% of sexual assaults are not reported crime – making rape one of the most under-rated crime. Furthermore, a staggering 90% of victims on campus do not report the rape crimes in the U.S.

These statistics have only proven that this major issue doesn't have enough awareness if the situation is still continuous and affecting a vast amount of peoples' lives. Therefore, it was a strong issue that I had wanted to mention within the novel, to bring alight and for people to speak about in. Similarly, another issue was psychological abuse.

Psychological abuse increases the trauma of physical and sexual abuse, and independently can cause long-term damage to a victim's mental health; in addition, studies have shown that subtle psychological abuse is much more harmful than overt psychological abuse or direct abuse, which was seen in two of the characters: Celeste and Bentley - "You'd be nothing without me."

The abuse includes humiliating, controlling, undermining the victim and much more. It may also include physical or sexual abuse which only multiples the damaging effects on the victim. It was a topic that's seen as a taboo and not very well talked about, especially as it's a form of abuse. I had felt that it was essential to bring this matter alight in the novel to bring recognition to warnings that show abuse to alert readers of the signs they must look out for during a relationship.

Additionally, I had mentioned the use of drugs, a substance that resulted in Scarlett's death. Overdose is a fairly common occurrence – more than 47,055 deaths due to overdose in the US (2014). As it is frequently used, especially with young adults – more than 10% of students in the U.S misuses amphetamine and 7% of high school seniors report misusing Adderall – it was a topic that needed to be mentioned to show the destructive effect on someone's health.

Scarlett's death had resulted due to the excessive drinking and the mixture of drugs, which her body was not able to handle, increasing her heartbeat and blood pressure, sending her body into overdrive. I personally felt that it was important to mention this within the novel, and how recklessly it can be used.

Many young adults use drugs as an escape, especially during times of stress, but then some are peered pressured into it, it was important to emphasise that situations like this exist and, although in the moment, drugs do seem to work, it will have an effect on your health in the long-term, sometimes in the short-term.

Furthermore, I had researched statutory rape, to able to shape Madeline's affair with her teacher, alongside harassment laws. I had studied New York laws and regulations, understanding how the judiciary system worked to corporate the knowledge into the novel; the research had benefitted the novel as the knowledge had helped accentuate the situation and had a more powerful impact overall.

The Elites was written to raise awareness about problematic issues faced in society that are not often spoken about. The main character, Candace, had faced difficult challenges, her grief and anger was a catalyst for initiating revenge; however, it had devastating consequences. The book analyses the

effects of grief, bullying and abuse of power on other people, and empha-
sises other issues faced in modern-day society. As a result, this book focuses
on challenging societal taboos and the destructive nature of power.